LOCKDOWN

L. DOUGLAS HOGAN
G. MICHAEL HOPF

DOOMSDAY

PRESS

PROLOGUE

FREDDY STOOD on the moonlit sidewalk, his gaze fixed on the street numbers nailed to the house in front of him. Rage filled his every fiber, he had questioned whether he should go, but here he was now. Yes, he could try to talk himself out of what needed to be done, but doing so would leave him haunted. No, there was no walking away from this. He had a thirst for revenge, and inside the house was the very thing that would quench that thirst.

Towering over him was a streetlamp, but gone was the typical yellowish glow. It, like the cars and most electronics, stood as a memory of the past, a relic of a time taken away in the blast of the super-EMP. In the days that had followed the attack, many thought the government would be there to protect them, to provide the much-needed comfort or resources for survival, but alas, they never came. People were left to fend for themselves, to find ways of surviving, and like Freddy, some were readjusting the scales of justice.

In the months before the attack, Freddy's life had been anything but normal. His life had been taken away only to be given back, and all due to the world ending; how odd was that? Now the only thing that stood between him and his new life was one man. This man was like the cars, as he represented a time gone by. It was impossible for Freddy to accept the new world without having complete closure of the old.

Tucked in his waistband was a Glock 19, the magazine fully loaded. Freddy pulled it out and held the pistol firmly in his hand. He admired it and liked how it felt in his grip. There was no need to press-check it; he knew there was a 9 mm round in the chamber. He had a plan. It was simple: slip in, find Antonio, and put a bullet in his head. A slight grin graced his face as he thought how easy it was to kill. It didn't take much effort, the simple squeezing of a trigger and boom, the bullet would explode out of the muzzle only to make impact with the flesh and deliver a fatal wound. Was killing Antonio like that, so easy, so painless, what he deserved? Or did this man who had caused him so much pain deserve another death, one that was slow and excruciating? He had his answer.

He slid the pistol back into his waistband and reached for a nine-inch sheath knife, "This will do," he said under his breath.

Without further hesitation, he stepped towards the house,

filled with determination. With each footfall, he drew closer and closer to ending his dreadful past and ushering in the new world with arms wide open.

1

OCTOBER 22, 2014

CHICAGO

FREDDY BECKER WAS the kid who learned to color inside the lines before everyone else. He was always the most studious and attentive to details and did well in school, yet he was never the teacher's pet. He left that degrading duty to the kids he called "the brown nosers."

During his junior year of high school, he attended a job fair, and there he spotted a booth that sparked an interest. The booth in question dealt with the criminal justice field, more specifically law. He knew upon examining the pamphlets and information that he wanted nothing else but to go into the world of crime fighting. He had visions of being that towering figure in the courtroom, the district attorney type, who would make the convincing case to the jury, which would result in them convicting the hardened criminals and sending them to where they belonged...behind bars.

But his enthusiasm waned after he graduated. The

thought of spending upwards of six plus years in school seemed impossible for him. It wasn't because he lacked the competence of learning or the brain power; no, it was because school was boring and slow. You see, Freddy had earned the nickname "Fritz" because he was so full of energy. He couldn't sit still for very long, so the thought of sitting in a courtroom or spending countless hours doing legal research was painful for him.

Even though the desire to be a lawyer had subsided, he still had a hunger to bring justice, right the wrong, and fight for the helpless. This led him towards the only other option, one that really was better suited for a man who didn't shy away from risk or bodily harm, a man who sought adventure and was never afraid to confront the bullies of the world. He wanted to be in the criminal justice field, and if he was still going to do it, his only option was to go directly into law enforcement itself and be a cop.

And so he did. He applied and eventually joined the ranks of the Chicago Police Department. He worked hard and had his share of dustups with the scourge of the lawless crowd that lurked in the city.

After five years he was still a patrolman, but he was undeterred. He loved the job and was in it for the long haul. It was then that he met Kaitlyn Browning, a beautiful college girl working on her master's degree in business administration. Their romance blossomed quickly; they fell in love and were married a year later. Not skipping a beat, the young newlyweds, both twenty-four, would conceive their first child,

Michael Allen, named after Kaitlyn's father, on their honeymoon. A year later, she was pregnant with Kayleigh Marie, named after Freddy's mom, now deceased. With two children and the additional expenses that went with young kids and a house that wasn't adequate, the Beckers needed more income, but like it had been for most of his life, luck was on Freddy's side.

Freddy's break came professionally a few years later. It was now 2014, and he went to work for the county as a parole officer. His new title meant that he had to supervise individuals who had served portions of their prison sentences before being released into *parole status*. Kaitlyn was a successful business administrator for the state of Illinois. Life couldn't have situated the two of them any better. He still had a high-stakes job that kept him on his toes, close to her family, which was what she wanted, and home at night to be with the kids; plus the physical output was demanding and just what he needed to keep his mind honed and focused.

It seemed like nothing could stop these two. Life was on a roll, they were healthy, happy, and they seemed unstoppable. But life has a way of reminding us that we can't have the good without the bad, and now it was time for Freddy to know just how bad it could get.

―――――

THE MORNING WAS as routine as any other workday morning. The alarm went off; he and Kaitlyn lay there for a couple of

minutes, rubbing their eyes and trying to convince themselves it was time to start again. Freddy was always out of bed
first, with Kaitlyn to follow. He made his way to the bathroom, and she to the kids' rooms.

Kaitlyn knocked on the door.

"Wakey, wakey," she said, flipping the light on.

Onto the next room.

Knock, knock, knock. "Wake up, Mikey. It's time for school,"
she said again, flipping on the lights.

"I don't wanna go," he said, pulling the sheets up over his
head.

"Well, I don't wanna go to work, yet here we are."

Michael let out a disgruntled groan, typical of an
eight-year-old.

Freddy walked out of the bathroom and met Kaitlyn, who
swapped spots with him. "You didn't stink it up, did you?"

"I was literally in there thirty seconds." Freddy knew she
was joking. Their sense of humor was always inappropriate.
It was Freddy's fault. His job made him callous to social
norms. That rubbed off on Kaitlyn over time – that and the
fact that she was a state employee.

Freddy went straight for the cereal on top of the refrigerator. It wasn't the sweet stuff, either. Freddy and Kaitlyn
enjoyed the naturally sweetened stuff like Raisin Bran. After
pouring himself a generous bowl of cereal, he sat down at the
kitchen table, picked up the television remote, and turned on
a local news channel.

"Preliminary casualty reports are still coming in from the

explosions that rocked the Soldier Field Stadium last night. The President of the United States will be taking questions later this morning regarding a recent announcement that the national threat level will remain at red, giving rise to the question, 'When will it end?'"

Walking out of the bathroom and knocking on the kids' doors again, Kaitlyn joined Freddy in the kitchen. "Any updates?"

"No, they said the tally hasn't come in or been released yet."

"I can't believe this is happening. This past month has been insane. It seems so surreal."

"The writing's been on the wall for years," he said, shoveling in a heaping spoonful of cereal.

"I know. I guess we just kept sticking our heads in the sand and pretending like nothing was wrong."

"Nine-eleven was like a rallying call to all Muslims that non-Islamic states are susceptible to Islamic extremism."

"But why us?" she asked.

"Because we're exceptional. In the jail system, the inmates have a pecking order. The *barn boss* is the biggest baddest inmate, who pretty much rules the roost. The new inmate, though – they are near the bottom of the hierarchy, right above pedophiles and women killers. Anybody who's been locked up before knows that there's one way to quickly establish yourself – walk right up to the barn boss and punch him square in the face."

"Yeah? How's that work for him?"

"If he survives, he'll have status, and other inmates will take him seriously. The US is kind of like that barn boss. The Taliban wanted to make a statement. They made one; we faltered – they paid for it. Now they have status. The only way to stop it is eradication," Freddy said, wiping a droplet of milk from his chin.

"How do you eradicate a religion?"

"You can't. That's why we have to adapt to living in this *new world*."

Kaitlyn knew Freddy's structured mindset would be the biggest obstacle in this new world. He loved rules. He needed them. He needed structure. It was the very reason he chose law enforcement as his livelihood. Everything in law is black and white. Right and wrong. It's all spelled out right there on the pages. All Freddy had to do was follow the law.

Michael finally walked out of his bedroom.

Freddy chugged down the milk from the bottom of his cereal bowl and went to the bathroom to brush his teeth.

Unable to listen to the depressing and droning newscaster any longer, Kaitlyn turned the channel and asked Michael, "What would you like to watch this morning, Mikey?"

"*The Grim Adventures of Billy and Mandy*," he replied.

Kaitlyn sighed. "Why do you like that silliness?"

Michael shrugged his shoulders and, with the typical dry attitude he displayed in the mornings, asked, "Can I have waffles for breakfast?"

"Sure." Kaitlyn stood up and saw Kayleigh was now

walking into the kitchen. "Hey, hon, do you want some waffles, too?"

Kayleigh nodded. She had the same morning saltiness that her brother had. Freddy and Kayleigh liked to blame each other, refusing to believe that either of them had passed the trait on to the kids.

Freddy left the bathroom and made his way to the bedroom, where he got dressed for work.

A large mirror was fitted to the dresser that Kaitlyn's parents had bought for them as a wedding gift. He used it every morning to fix his hair, ensuring each hair was in place so that he looked presentable. Freddy believed that an officer's first line of defense was his presence. He took care to make sure he earned it.

His shirt was a wrinkle-free polo shirt with an embroidered badge. Since he had a badge displayed on his shirt, he was fully authorized to carry a service pistol on his hip. He kept that on the top shelf of his bedroom closet, out of the reach of his kids. His choice of firearm was a Glock model 22. It shot a .40-caliber round – plenty of stopping power for any two-legged critters, as he'd sometimes say. For slacks, Freddy liked to wear khaki-colored tactical pants with cargo pockets. This gave him a professional appearance with maneuverability and practicality.

Finally dressed, he gave himself a once-over in the mirror, then rejoined Kaitlyn and the kids in the kitchen.

Kaitlyn's job started a half hour later than his, so she got to spend more time waking up than he did.

With a content smile, Freddy gazed at his family. He liked to take his life in before he departed each morning. He just never knew if it would be his last. If Freddy was anything, it was grateful. He never wanted to ever leave without taking a mental snapshot of them all. He kissed Kaitlyn goodbye, messed up Michael's hair, and gave Kayleigh a peck on the cheek. "Love you," he said to them all.

"Love you, too," they replied in unison.

After one more look, Freddy turned and exited the house.

———

FREDDY SHARED office space with Ryan Pettigrew, a fellow parole agent and longtime friend. Ryan almost always beat Freddy to the office and had the door unlocked and the coffee going.

The first thing Freddy would do when he arrived was to banter with Ryan. He enjoyed the back-and-forth. After a few minutes of that, he'd shift into work mode, sit down at his computer, and get to work.

Today wasn't any different. As he waited for his computer to boot up, he stared at the family photo that sat next to the monitor. In the photo were Kaitlyn, Michael, and Kayleigh, big smiles on their faces. He recalled that day and just how happy they had been when the photo was taken. Each time he glanced at it, it brought him warmth; it was undoubtedly his favorite family photo.

"You gonna stare at that thing all day?" Ryan asked.

Freddy laughed. "I know, I'm a sap."

"I'm the same way," Ryan said, turning his own family photo to face Freddy. "See? Janie, Ricky and Randy were all in good moods that day."

"What's up with you and the letter *R*?"

"Eh, my dad's name was Richard. His dad's name was Robert."

Freddy rolled his eyes. "Geesh. When will you be required to recycle a name or two?"

"I know. I'm a sap, too."

Freddy looked back to his computer screen, but it was still going through the slow boot-up. He was anxious to get the drug test results from the county on the parolees he was responsible for. Being that they came in the early morning gave him ample time to drop in on his parolees and build a case against them if he needed to.

Annoyed by how slow his computer was, he got up and filled his coffee cup. He wondered who would be on the drug report.

An audible melody of music from the Windows operating system told him the computer was ready to go. He strutted over, sat down and opened his e-mail account. A few seconds later the e-mails began to populate the screen, with the one he was looking for near the top.

Across from him, Ryan was already reading his reports.

With a click of his mouse, he opened the e-mail and began to read the report, to find a familiar name, Antonio De LaRosa. He wasn't surprised to see his name and that they'd found trace amounts of THC in his urine, meaning Antonio had broken a condition of his parole.

"Antonio, Antonio, you just couldn't keep it clean, could you?" Freddy smirked.

South Side, Chicago

Antonio De LaRosa was the twenty-three-year-old son of illegal immigrants Juan and Maria De LaRosa. In the late '80s, his parents were coyoted into the United States from Mexico, eventually settling down in Chicago. Antonio was born in 1991. He wasn't a bad kid growing up, especially in his younger years, but his behavior continued to deteriorate as he struggled in school academically, primarily because he had a tough time grasping English, and the school systems didn't provide support.

By the time Antonio was in high school, most of his friends were affiliated with gangs, and his desire to do well in school had all but evaporated. He was often invited to join gangs, but the murder rate in South Deering was high, which struck fear in him, but it was mainly his father, who advocated against such affiliations.

The day before his dad was shot and killed by a stray bullet, he told Antonio, *"Tony, the greatest pain you can bring to this family is to take part in that violence. Whatever you do in this life, please don't bring your family shame."* Juan's comment was directly tied to the gang violence that was ravaging South Deering. The only reason they even stayed was because of the hope and promise that the neighborhood was going to clean up. It never did.

After his father was killed, Antonio dropped out of high school to take on odd jobs to help support his aging mother, but these jobs weren't normal. Sometimes he would find himself acting as a courier for drugs. The gangbangers used him because he had no active membership with them. The problem with the courier job was that it originally paid him a few bucks, but later turned into non-cash payments of marijuana. That only served to dim Antonio's already short foresight. What could he do? He couldn't tell them *no.* Once he was tied to the criminal activities, the gangs knew Antonio would have to accept any payment made to him. He was stuck.

A bit of time went by and Antonio was still working here and there; then something horrible happened: his mother had a stroke. Unable to meet the medical expenses, and fearing he'd lose her, Antonio looked to gangbanger friends for a solution. They refused to involve themselves unless he would *blood in*, which was the practice of taking a beating or committing a violent offense to get accepted into the gang. If he did that, they promised, he and his mother would be taken care of. To get in, Antonio would be given a choice. Either take a severe beating or perform a series of tasks to prove his allegiance to the gang. Taking a beating wouldn't work, since he had to actively care for his mother, so he opted to commit violent acts on behalf of the gang.

Antonio was arrested on his very first task – an armed

robbery of a local convenience store. As luck would have it, the storeowner knew Antonio's mother and father and chose not to press charges, but the state's attorney saw it differently. Ultimately, the judge considered Antonio's lack of a criminal past and sentenced him to six years.

Since the Illinois criminal justice system allowed for a day-for-day exchange of time for good behavior, Antonio hoped to meet release criteria after serving only three years of his sentence; however, the judge who oversaw his case modified the provisions and allowed him to be paroled after two years, providing he abstained from all drug use and gang-related activity and would care for his ailing mother. Had the judge not been contacted by the storeowner, who knew Maria was in bad health, Antonio would likely have served out his time.

"Good morning, Mama," Antonio said, entering the living room. The sunlight was already cascading through the front window of the apartment. Antonio opened the windows to let in even more sunlight, then turned to face her. Something was wrong. Different. Maria's face was sagging on one side, and her arm was hanging over the edge of the recliner. She couldn't speak, either. Fearing the worst, Antonio raced to her aid.

"Mama? Mama, what do I do?" he asked as he fumbled around, not knowing what to do.

She didn't answer his pleas verbally, but a cry for help could be visibly seen in her eyes.

He immediately grabbed his cell phone. "Don't worry, Mama. I'm gonna call for help."

FREDDY MADE it a priority to drop in unannounced on his parolees. The way he saw it, this helped him keep the parolees on their toes. If they knew he was coming, they'd clean up their act and never get caught breaking the rules of their probation. It was early, by Antonio's standards, and Freddy knew that at this time of day, Antonio was always home.

The second he pulled up to the front of the De LaRosa residence, he noticed their car wasn't there.

"Hmm, where are you, Tony?" Freddy asked out loud.

Freddy looked around. All the gangbangers who would normally line the streets and corners of the neighborhood weren't even out of bed yet. Their illegal activities kept them awake well into the night. This lifestyle made the Chicago neighborhoods safest in the early morning hours.

Freddy called dispatch to let the department know where he was. Once they acknowledged, he exited the safety of his car and walked up to the De LaRosa home.

With a search warrant in hand, Freddy opened the front door and peeked into the apartment. It seemed quiet, and there was no sign of either Antonio or his mother. Looking at the recliner in the front room, it was apparent that somebody was living in the chair. He walked past the front room and announced himself. "Antonio De LaRosa, this is Agent Becker. Are you here?"

There was no answer.

Freddy continued the search of the apartment. He kept smelling a hint of cannabis in the air, but he couldn't pinpoint the location. He made his way to Antonio's bedroom and was about to call a K-9 unit when he looked in the trash can.

"Got you!" he exclaimed.

Freddy took pictures of the trash can, just as he had discovered it, then pulled the entire liner out. He left the apartment with the evidence and returned to his office.

Advocate Trinity Hospital, South Side, Chicago

Antonio was nervously waiting to hear something from the physicians. They hadn't let him accompany his mother into the intensive care unit, and not hearing a word gave him a bad feeling that things were much worse than he had thought. She had completely bypassed the usual ER check-in and had gone straight to ICU. He would have been happy to hear anything at all.

A couple of hours passed before a doctor finally came out and met Antonio.

"Are you Mr. De LaRosa?" the physician asked.

"I am. How's my mother?"

"I'm afraid your mother suffered a massive stroke sometime in the night. The stroke has worsened her already weakened condition," the physician said before pausing.

"And?" Antonio pressed.

"She had another one as she was being prepped for review. I'm afraid that your mother is in very serious condition, and we're going to have to hold her for a while."

Antonio was left speechless.

Seeing how shocked Antonio was, the doctor gave him something to keep his mind occupied and to prepare him for the worst. "Mr. De LaRosa, the best thing you can do for your mother at this point is to go set her affairs in order. I'm sorry to have to give you news like this. It's hard to know if she's going to be able to recover from something so serious. If she has a couple more strokes, or even one more, I'm afraid she may not survive."

Antonio tried to hold it together. His eyes welled with tears, and his mind went completely blank. He felt nothing but numbness in his head.

"Mr. De LaRosa?" the doctor said, hoping to get a response.

Antonio didn't answer. He ignored the doctor, spun around, and raced out of the hospital in a panic.

FREDDY WAS RETURNING from the state's attorney's office when he saw Antonio pacing back and forth in front of the hospital.

He grabbed his radio to contact dispatch and let them know he was about to make a stop on one of his parolees for a violation. He gave them his exact location just in case something went bad.

Freddy parked the car in the first available spot he could find, then went after his prey. To catch up to him, he darted across the street, straight through the dense noontime traffic, and up behind Antonio, who was still pacing. It was clear to Freddy that Antonio seemed a bit frantic, as he was even mumbling to himself.

"De LaRosa!" Freddy barked just feet away.

Antonio heard his name, turned and saw Freddy standing feet from him. *Not now, man,* he thought. He then noticed the look in Freddy's eyes. Something was wrong. He thought about making a run for it but was still partially in shock from the news about his mother.

Freddy reached for his cuffs.

No, c'mon, man, Antonio thought, then did what came naturally...ran.

Freddy gave chase.

As he sprinted away, Antonio began to realize his gut reaction probably wasn't the correct one, as running would only land him back behind bars and make him look guilty, of what, he didn't know just yet.

"Tony, stop. You're only going to make this worse!" Freddy shouted.

Antonio took heed and stopped. He threw his arms into the air and waited for Freddy to catch up.

Freddy caught up, grabbed Antonio's right arm, and barked, "You wanna run, Tony? Look where that landed you! Right into my custody." He pulled his right arm back, then his left, and slipped the cuffs on them.

"Why you arrestin' me, man?"

"I knew you couldn't swing a real man's life out here, Tony."

"What are you talkin' about?"

"Your drug tests came back positive, *mi amigo*. You're using, and that's a violation of your parole." Freddy purposely didn't tell Antonio about the marijuana he'd found in his bedroom. Not telling him gave him an edge for his case against Antonio's parole.

"I haven't smoked any dope since I been out, man. You gotta believe me. I'm tellin' you the truth!"

"Tell it to the judge."

Freddy spun Antonio around and escorted him back to his car.

"Please, Agent Becker, please don't do this. My mama is in the hospital, and she needs my help."

Freddy was sorry to hear that Antonio's mom was ill, but he felt obliged to do the right thing, and that was to follow the letter of the law. "I'm sorry, Tony, but you know the rules and you broke them."

"I didn't though, Agent Becker. I promise. It might look like I did, but I didn't break the rules. I'm being straight with you. Please. Please don't do this. My mom's gonna need me to care for her," Antonio pleaded.

"I'm sure your mom will be looked after, Tony. Everybody likes her. She's a good woman. She'll be taken care of."

"Agent Becker! Man! You gotta listen to me and quit bein' so hard on people. One of these days you're gonna need someone to go light on you, and then you'll understand what I'm sayin'."

"This ain't one of those days, Tony. You were given a chance and you blew it," Freddy said. He opened the right rear door and put Antonio inside. He buckled him in tightly; then as he closed the door, he said, "You just couldn't go straight, could you, not even for your dear mom?"

Beaten and unable to convince Agent Becker to be lenient, Antonio sat with his head hung low.

2

OCTOBER 27, 2014
CHICAGO

ANTONIO SAT QUIETLY POISED in the courtroom as he waited for Judge Warfeld to enter. To say he was nervous would be an understatement. The sweat that continuously beaded on his forehead stood in contrast to the dryness of his throat. Each time he swallowed, it felt like he was going to choke. His gaze was transfixed on the judge's empty chair. Soon it would be filled, and when that came, so would his fate.

Behind him sat dozens of reporters and witnesses. He kept looking over his shoulder to see if maybe his mom would be there despite the status of her health, but each time he turned to look, he would find her not there. He scanned the faces, but not one was familiar. He was surrounded by strangers in an all too familiar setting. Then he caught sight of Freddy. So he wasn't without one face he knew.

He gave Freddy a scowl, then fixed his gaze on the state's attorney just in front of Freddy, his desk orderly with folders stacked neatly in front of him. The contents of those folders held the evidence, the state's case on why he should be sent back to jail.

The jury box was empty. This would be a bench ruling. Antonio kept hoping that Judge Warfeld's respect for Maria would win the day, because the problem wasn't going to be the weight of evidence. Antonio knew that Becker didn't have to prove his guilt beyond a reasonable doubt. This wasn't a criminal case. This was a parole hearing, and all the judge needed to send him back to prison was enough evidence to show that the offense was more likely to have happened than not to have – and Agent Becker had a great service record. Nobody would believe a high school dropout over a decorated police officer. If Judge Warfeld oversaw the case, De LaRosa might get lucky with a warning or, worst-case scenario, another modification to his parole.

"All rise!" the bailiff yelled. Antonio stood up. His knees grew weak as he waited, impatiently, to see the judge's face. "The honorable Judge Schnoeker will be presiding."

Antonio's heart plummeted to the deepest parts of his chest. He tried to hold it together. Everybody who was anybody had heard of Judge Dennis Schnoeker. He was a hard-nosed straight shooter who failed to see the gray in any law-related matter. He believed in the letter of the law, and even God Himself would have to pay him a personal visit to teach him clemency. He was as strict as strict could be, giving no slack to mercy as far as the law was concerned. Rumor was, this judge once convicted a family friend for no other reason than to prove he wouldn't let associations govern his rulings.

For Antonio, this meant mandatory prison time. He would carry out the remainder of his sentence in the big house. That was bad news in and of itself, but even worse was the news that his sick mother would be alone. Antonio had no siblings, and his last relative in Mexico had recently died. The only thing worse would be his mother's passing. That would be something he wouldn't be able to cope with.

For Freddy, the judge's presence meant a sure conviction, making him feel confident knowing that his work would be paying off.

"You may be seated," the judge said.

The courtroom was brought to session.

"I've reviewed the case against Mr. De LaRosa. There's not a lot of room to argue with the evidence at hand. After thoroughly going over every piece of data regarding Mr. De LaRosa's case, it would seem that this court has been very lenient on him. I'm going to ask the state's attorney and Mr. De LaRosa's counsel to approach the bench."

Antonio's lawyer was a public defender by the name of Rudolph Chadwick. He didn't place too much effort into the case against his client. He knew the hearing would be a bench ruling, and there wasn't much of a chance for his client to get off the hook. The best he could hope for was leniency.

The state's attorney was a man by the name of Preston Wolfe. He was serving his second term in his elected position.

Preston and Rudolph approached the judge.

"Good morning, Your Honor," each of them said to Judge Schnoeker.

"I don't see any reason to prolong this matter," the judge said. "I've read the testimony provided by Agent Becker, and in his statement, he recorded that he found cannabis in the bedroom of the defendant." Judge Schnoeker looked at Rudolph. "Is this accurate?"

"It is, Your Honor."

"Then the matter is concluded."

Agent Becker was trying to read the lips as the judge spoke. His voice was barely audible. To his left, the recorder was paused and waiting for the next official word to record. Preston and Chadwick returned to their seats. Antonio's lawyer didn't even make eye contact with his client. It was that body language that told Freddy what he wanted to know. In just a moment, his suspicions would be confirmed.

"Mr. De LaRosa," the judge said.

Antonio stood up.

"It's the court's decision that you be remanded to the Cook County Jail until such time as we find a correctional center where you will carry out the remainder of your sentence, which I have found to be four years. It is also the court's ruling that you receive an additional year for betraying the court's good graces and violating your parole." The judge threw down his gavel, and the bailiff ordered court security to escort Antonio out.

The security guards approached and took hold of Antonio. Now that the fear of the judge's ruling was past him,

Antonio turned to look at Freddy. "You should've went loose on me, Becker."

Freddy heard the inmate's words, but he'd been threatened a hundred times over by men worse than Antonio. He wasn't intimidated. Freddy just kept his head down and collected his case files. As he was walking out of the courtroom, he turned to look at Antonio one last time. Antonio was looking over his shoulder at Freddy as the guards walked him through the door that would lead to his holding cell. Before he disappeared, he said one last thing to Freddy. "If anything happens to my mama, you'll live to regret it."

Freddy thought nothing of it. He didn't like the idea that Antonio's mother was in the hospital, and took no pleasure in knowing she couldn't care for herself. Like Judge Schnoeker, Freddy was a man of the law, and in their minds, there was very little wriggle room. The physical condition of Maria De LaRosa was unfortunate, but to Freddy, her health should have no bearing on the weight of his job performance. Freddy simply lacked the capacity to carry the weight of everyone else's problems on his own back. Life was just easier when the law spelled out everything in black and white.

3

NOVEMBER 1, 2014
COOK COUNTY JAIL, CHICAGO

It was lunchtime at Cook County Jail, and all the inmates were walking in a single-file line to the chow hall. The rules were simple – stay in line, keep your hands to yourself, and be quiet. Violating these rules pushed the possibility of getting caught by the correctional officers, or COs as they were called, and ticketed for breaking them. At mealtimes, the inmates were called to the chow hall by their assigned unit. Antonio was assigned to Baker Unit.

Antonio walked slowly and quietly in line as the men in front of and behind him shuffled their feet until they arrived at the serving line.

Upon arriving, he was met with the usual vulgarity and catcalls from the seasoned inmates. As luck would have it, he didn't have any real issues reintegrating with general population. It might have been more difficult, but thankfully some old friends from the last time he was incarcerated were still on Baker Unit. Not only that, it just so happened that the same gang that was running his 'hood back home had members in Baker.

Deep down, Antonio didn't want anything to do with gang activity. Gangs meant the real possibility of doing a longer sentence. His mom was still ill, and all he could think of was her and getting out. He didn't have the mental energy or focus necessary to meet the gang's expectations. They wanted him. Why wouldn't they? In the big house, every additional member strengthens the gang's influence. The more influence they have, the more power they have. Power equals control. And right now, Antonio wasn't feeling like he had control of anything.

There weren't any real worries from the inmates working the serving line. Those were the best-behaved prisoners. Work was a coveted thing in prison. Getting off the cellblock and staying busy with your hands helped to push time along a little quicker. The servers kept their noses down and focused on their work. That didn't mean they weren't paying attention.

"Hey, man," the voice of an inmate behind him whispered.

Antonio knew the man by name. It was Rodrigo Carbolla. He was a respected and well-known street enforcer for the Latin Kings, who used to live near his neighborhood.

"Hey, man, listen," Rodrigo said, following closely behind

Antonio. "You can't keep avoiding this. You're gonna need us soon. Just remember that."

"I can't be gettin' hooked on any issues, man," Antonio answered, trying to hide any signs of weakness by using a commanding voice. "I need to get out of here. My mom was very sick when I got picked up."

"You join us, and we'll watch out for your mom. We know where you're from. South Deering, right?"

Antonio held his tray out to the server. "Salisbury steak," he said, pretending to ignore the street enforcer.

"Man, you play like you ain't hearing me, but I know your mom needs to be watched out for until you finish your time," Rodrigo said to Antonio.

Antonio scooted along, trying to ignore him, but Rodrigo was relentless.

"Green beans," Antonio said, holding his tray up to the next server. The line of inmates continued to scoot along.

"You know where to find me if you change your mind," Rodrigo whispered.

Tired of the incessant harassment, Antonio raised his voice. "I told you *no!*"

It was just loud enough for the COs to hear.

"Is there a problem, De LaRosa?" the CO asked.

Antonio stared down Rodrigo, then answered, "No! No problem, CO."

"Keep that line moving, then," the CO commanded.

Antonio continued and filled his tray. When he was done,

he sat down and ate his meal with no further issues, but the pressure was there. Could he avoid it for much longer if they kept prying? He didn't know, but what he did know was that he couldn't chance any undue slipups. All he cared about was getting out and getting home to his mother.

4

NOVEMBER 2, 2014
COOK COUNTY JAIL, CHICAGO

SITTING on the edge of his bed in his darkened cell, Antonio did his best praying that all would work out and he'd see his mother again.

All he cared about had been left behind in the intensive care unit that fateful day he'd been arrested by Freddy. He had sent fifteen letters addressed to both the hospital and his home, just in case she was discharged, yet he'd not received a word, nothing. It was the lack of communication that he found torturous.

He had no contact with his mother and had no idea what her condition was, making him fear the worst. He tried everything from calling advocacy groups to asking gangbangers if they'd mind sending a person over to check on her, yet his pleas for help went unheeded and unanswered. He was alone. A man with no home and possibly on the cusp of losing his last blood relative.

As he sat pondering his next move, he contemplated caving to Rodrigo's requests. Maybe then he'd get at the minimum the support he needed to know just how she was doing. He hated knowing that was possibly his only option, but what else could he do? Desperation sometimes leads the hearts of men into dark places.

Antonio walked out of his cell. As he went down the heavily worn stairs, the railing discolored from countless hands, he knew what he had to do. He entered the dayroom and scanned the space, looking for the one man he now believed could help him.

The dayroom was filled with small metal tables, all bolted to the floor. Each table had four seats, also bolted to the floor and welded to the table. This was done to prevent them from being thrown or used as weapons.

As his eyes surveilled the room, they stopped when he spotted Rodrigo, who was sitting with other members of the Latin Kings. With confidence in his plan, he approached.

"What's up, *jefe*?" Rodrigo bantered.

"I'll do it," Antonio said, looking over his shoulder to the control room.

"Don't worry about them. They can't hear what we're saying."

"No, but they can see our associations," Antonio reminded him.

"If you really want in, you need to stop worrying about what they think. They don't hassle us," Rodrigo quipped, his fingers cradling playing cards. He looked at the others and said, "Give me a second with him."

Ever obedient, the men stood and walked away. "Have a seat, *jefe*. You've got my ears. Say what's on your mind," Rodrigo said, his tone subdued.

"I'll join, but I need something in return," Antonio said, his fingers clasped together on the table in front of him.

"Listen to me carefully, De LaRosa. You don't come to us with demands. If you want in, we give the demands to you. You see how that works?"

"Just tell me what you need," Antonio replied defiantly.

"We need you to off Enrique."

The demand was high. Enrique was Antonio's cellmate. It would be difficult to kill him without giving himself away.

"Why Enrique?"

"Didn't you just hear what I said? You're not in charge. I am. If you're gonna do this, you're gonna be a follower – a soldier. You do what you're told. You understand?"

"What if I get caught?"

"Then you'll do some time in segregation. You already know what else will happen."

"They'll add to my time."

"That's right." Rodrigo looked at Antonio's face. He was deep in thought. He could tell Antonio was desperate. "Tell you what. You tell us what you need, and after you off Enrique, we'll take care of you whether you get caught or not."

Antonio thought about it. "Deal! When I got picked up,

my mother was in ICU. She hasn't been replying to any of my letters. I've been sending them home and to the hospital. Nothing! I need her checked on."

Rodrigo nodded his head in agreement. "Done."

Antonio stood up and left. There was no handshake, no cordial words of departure. Just business.

Becker Residence, Chicago

Freddy pulled into the driveway. He was happy to be home; he sighed and took in his home. He always made a mental note to never take his life for granted and to have gratitude for the things he did have even if his workday was typical, like today was. Nothing out of the ordinary. A few checkups, a few check-ins, and an arrested parolee. All in a good day's work, but still, he knew at any moment shit could go sideways.

As usual, Kaitlyn had beat him home and greeted him at the door with a kiss. "How was work?"

"More of the same."

"Yeah? How many did Big Daddy put away today?"

"One," he answered with a sigh.

"What's wrong, then? Isn't that what you shoot for every day?"

"I just don't understand. These guys do bad things. They get caught. They get their sentence. They meet parole. They take advantage of the system; then they wind up back behind bars. It all seems so nonsensical."

"Consider it job security. If the system's broke, they have you to bring balance."

"Yeah, I guess."

"You could always go lighter on them and give them a second or a third chance," she suggested.

"What good would that do? We'd have no checks and balances, and the crime rate would be astronomical."

"It seems that no matter what you do, you're unhappy with it."

"I'm just –"

"You're bored again, aren't you?" she asked, rubbing his shoulders.

"It just seems like there should be something more to life."

The kids came running in from outside. They were screaming at each other and running for the freezer. Their backpacks were dropped in the middle of the front room as they fought for the last drumstick ice-cream cone.

"What could be better than this?" she joked. "Besides, Ryan called."

"Really? What'd he want?"

"He asked for you. I told him you weren't home yet. He should know this. You have the same office space, right? Anyway, he said he was being harassed by some gangsters about an arrest he made the other night. Apparently, his family's lives have been threatened. Ryan's your best friend. If you're thinking about a transfer over issues of boredom, just focus on him. Maybe you can help him out and get the punks harassing him off his back."

"You're right. Me and Ryan have known each other since the police academy, and we've shared the same office space for a while now, too. I'll have him over for a cookout. That'll get his mind off things."

"Just remember to invite his family."

"He probably hasn't mentioned anything to his kids. So try not to bring it up in front of them."

"I've got your back, Agent Becker," she said, giggling as she kissed his lips.

Cook County Jail, Chicago

Antonio spent the afternoon sharpening a toothbrush he stole from another inmate's commissary. He wasn't trying to be too sophisticated with the shank. He rubbed it on the concrete floor to give it a tip, then wrapped an old shoelace around the handle for a grip.

Enrique was an older inmate, about fifty years of age. He had been good to Antonio and was always sharing with him stories of his childhood and where he went wrong in life. The intention behind it was to steer Antonio down the right path. Enrique was more of a mentor to Antonio than a cellmate. He had served thirty-five years of a life sentence for murder. That was what Antonio used for justification to his conscience. Enrique was a murderer. He took somebody's life for selfish reasons; now Antonio would take his.

It would be a simple stabbing. Wait for the predetermined distraction, then make his move, and that would be suppertime. The kitchen and dining hall would be loaded with inmates, and only two guards would be on duty. The distraction to lure the guards away was set; two gangs would start a fight.

Antonio stood behind Enrique in the chow line, his heart pumping, and cool sweat beaded on his brow. He knew that soon the distraction would kick off.

A ruckus erupted in the corner of the dining hall.

Antonio snapped his head in the direction of the fight, as did everyone else.

The guards reacted appropriately, giving the opportunity that Antonio needed.

There was no time to think, he needed to act, and act he did. Antonio crouched down, slid his right hand into his sock, and wrapped his fingers around the shank. The blood in his veins was pumping and his heart raced. This was it, this was his moment. To back out now meant he'd be the next target, and nobody would check on his mother.

All eyes turned towards the ruckus, including Enrique's.

Doors burst open as other guards came running in.

"You seeing this?" Enrique chirped, not knowing what was about to happen.

With the shank firmly in his grip, Antonio made his move. Without a second's hesitation, he plunged the shank deep into the neck of Enrique.

A startled Enrique jumped and reached towards the wound.

Antonio withdrew the shank and again plunged it in, this time going fully into Enrique's already bleeding neck. He repeated this move several more times.

Enrique gasped and toppled to the floor, blood pouring from the numerous wounds. Enrique had little time to fight back. It happened so fast. He managed to look Antonio in his eyes as he was dying. He couldn't speak, but his eyes were asking why.

Not retreating from his attack, Antonio kept stabbing over and over. He couldn't allow Enrique to live; he had to make sure he was dead.

Lying in a pool of dark red blood, Enrique's body twitched, no doubt just his nervous system still reacting, but there was no doubt he was dead.

Antonio's mind went numb. He lost emotion in that moment. Respect for human life was gone as he stared into Enrique's lifeless gaze and dropped the shank.

Blood was everywhere. Especially on Antonio, which could only mean he'd be pegged for the murder. He had to cover it up, but how? The men near him had spread out, leaving only him and Enrique's dead body on the floor.

What do I do? Antonio thought. He hadn't planned this part. His eyes widened when an idea came to mind.

"Help!" Antonio screamed.

A guard looked his way and saw Antonio waving.

Antonio dropped to his knees and attempted to resuscitate Enrique. His plan was to make it look like he was helping and that the real murderer got away.

The guard approached, looked at Enrique's body then to Antonio. "What happened?"

"I'm in line when I hear that fight over there; then I see him on the ground," Antonio replied.

"Did you see who did it?" the guard asked.

"No."

The guard looked at the other inmates and asked the same question.

Almost in unison, the others shook their heads and said they hadn't seen anything.

The other fight had been broken up, and more guards approached.

A second guard asked, "Who did it?"

The first guard shook his head.

"Oh, let me guess, no one knows," the second guard quipped.

Antonio took this as his cue and stepped back. He slowly disappeared into the crowd.

SITTING ALONE IN A NEW CELL, far from general population, Antonio could only think someone had snitched on him or that his plan to look innocent had failed. Either way, he was out of general population and no closer to knowing the status of his mother.

Footfalls echoed as they approached his cell. Antonio looked out and saw a guard. "De LaRosa."

"What's up, CO?" Antonio asked.

"Here's the supper you didn't get to eat. Enjoy. Make sure you drink your milk!" The guard smirked before he walked off.

Make sure I drink my milk?

He lifted the milk carton and saw a small newspaper article. It was a cutout from the obituary section of the papers. His heart skipped a beat. It was Antonio's worst nightmare.

"Maria De LaRosa, of Chicago, Illinois, passed away October 28, 2014, at..." Antonio couldn't read any further.

"No!" he said, his head in his hands; tears flowed easily. "No!"

His grief went directly to rage. He stood up, clenched his fist, and drove it into the concrete wall. "I'll kill you; I'll fucking kill you for what you did!"

5

NOVEMBER 3, 2014
COOK COUNTY JAIL, CHICAGO

"WARDEN SAID Internal Security didn't have anything on you. You're outta here," Correctional Officer Dailey said. The CO took a position just outside Antonio's cell door and unlocked the chuckhole he'd been receiving his meals through. Officer Dailey lowered his body to investigate the inside of the cell, to find Antonio sitting with his face in his hands.

"What's wrong, Tony? I just gave you some good news. You're going back to general pop!"

Antonio didn't move.

Dailey secured the chuckhole and opened the door, flooding the cell with near blinding light.

Antonio looked up. His eyes were red and puffy.

"Hey, man. You eat something you're allergic to?"

Antonio didn't respond. He just stood up and stepped out of his cell.

The guard secured the door and led Antonio to the dayroom in general population.

Antonio stepped inside, scanned the room, and found the man he wanted to see, Rodrigo. He walked over and stood without saying a word.

"You did good, *jefe*!" Rodrigo said, almost in a congratulatory mindset.

"You remember that pig who arrested me?" Antonio asked.

Rodrigo could see something was different with Antonio. Something darker. "Yeah, man. You got a bum deal. I'm sorry to hear about your mom. I know how much she meant to you – how much she meant to the community."

"She meant everything to me."

Looking closer, Rodrigo could see an absence of light in Antonio's eyes. They looked hollow. Almost empty. Like he'd lost his soul. "You okay, *jefe*? I know seg can do a number on a man, but you weren't in there very long. We threatened the witnesses. Nobody's gonna talk. We kept you clean. We took care of you, just like I promised."

Antonio kept staring at him with his empty gaze. "I'm all in. My mom's gone. I got nothing else to live for. I got one more request and this gang can have my very life."

Rodrigo studied his eyes again. "Yeah. I believe you. What you want?"

"Not *want*. Need!"

"I'm listening," Rodrigo said as his tongue licked his lips in anticipation of what the request would be.

"I want Agent Freddy Becker to pay for what he's done. I'm not talking death, either. I want him to suffer like I've suffered. Take his family, take their lives, like he did mine. Spare his life, though. That part's important. He needs to live with the loss."

"That's cold, *jefe*. That man didn't kill your mom."

"You're not listening. I want him to pay. I want him to suffer, do you understand?" Antonio growled.

Rodrigo had never seen Antonio like this; in fact, it impressed him as well as struck some fear in him. Nothing is more terrifying than a man with nothing to live for. "Okay. I got this," he said then stood. "You did good, real good." He turned and walked away, leaving Antonio alone with his thoughts.

6

NOVEMBER 8, 2014

BECKER RESIDENCE, CHICAGO

FREDDY'S BACKYARD was awash in the orange glow of the bonfire, and feet away the aroma of various meats grilling on the barbeque filled the air. And to top it all off, the cooler next to his seat was filled with his favorite beer.

Freddy opened it, pulled out a longneck, and handed it to Ryan.

"Thanks, man," Ryan said with a timid grin. A couple of days prior, Ryan had contacted Freddy and asked to talk to him about his gangbanger issues and how his family was being harassed.

Happy to oblige, Freddy had invited him over. He thought it was ironic that Kaitlyn had just brought up the idea to do something with Ryan to help stay focused. He loved grilling, so it only seemed natural to have him and his family over for a cookout.

"Can't thank you enough for having me over, Becker,"

Ryan said. On the police force, everybody addressed each other by their last names. It became so habitual that even off-duty they found themselves doing it.

"No problem, Pettigrew," he said, chuckling beneath his breath.

Ryan smiled back then looked over at his wife, Janie, and saw that she was at ease chitchatting with Kaitlyn. "It's good to see Janie smiling again," he said.

Freddy glanced in the same direction and said, "Yeah, man. It stinks that the department hasn't managed to do something more for you and your family. I mean, how'd those thugs even find out where you live? How'd they get your address?"

"I'm not sure. Personally, I think there's a mole in our department."

The comment caught Freddy's attention. "A mole?"

"Yeah. I mean, think about it. No sooner than I stop a small-time drug ring that they know my number and my address? How does that happen? Who cares about a bunch of no-name drug runners? There's gotta be somebody on the inside."

"Hmm," Freddy mused as he got up and went to the barbeque. He picked up the spatula and began flipping the burger patties. "God, I hope you're wrong about this."

"I could be, but I doubt it."

"If there's somebody on the inside, then there's nothing keeping my family safe either. Heck, no one is safe." Freddy looked over at Kaitlyn and then at Kayleigh and Michael as they played with Ryan's kids. "If anything ever happens to my family – if they're ever threatened in any way, I don't know what I'll do."

"You'll become the man you need to be to protect them. That's all we can do, right? I mean, protecting our family is our first duty," Ryan said, looking to Freddy for confirmation.

"Absolutely, Pettigrew. I'd do anything for my family. I know you would, too."

It was the confirmation Ryan was looking for. "Say, you wouldn't mind if I used your bathroom, would you?"

Freddy looked at Ryan again. "Are you serious? You don't have to ask me for permission to use my bathroom. Get on it!"

With beer in hand, Ryan started walking toward the back entrance to Freddy's house.

"Go on, now!" Freddy bantered. "Go drop the kids off at the pool."

Ryan laughed. "I'm dropping your kids off at the pool," he said, entering the house.

Kaitlyn and Janie looked over and saw Freddy was alone at the grill.

"Do you mind if I go thank your husband?" Janie asked Kaitlyn.

"Thank him for what?"

"For having us over and for talking to Ryan. I'm sure you know what's been going on."

"You go ahead," Kaitlyn said and gave her a nod.

Janie hopped up and walked over to the barbeque, her drink gently cradled in her hands. "Heya, Becker."

"Hey, Janie. Are you having a good time?"

"Yasss! That's what I wanted to come thank you for. Ryan's head has been in the clouds lately. He worries so much about me and the kids that he can't even enjoy family time. This is the first time I've seen him smile in a long while. Actually, it's the first time we've been out in a while as a family."

Freddy smiled.

"What?" she asked, curious about his smile

"Oh, nothing. That's just what he said about you."

"Yeah, we haven't been very happy lately. He tried keeping it from me for a while, but you know how it is with Kaitlyn. If you're hiding something from her, she's sure to find out what it is in time. In any case, I just wanted to say thanks."

"You're welcome. Anytime, anytime at all. Say, how's work going at the hospital?"

Janie was a nurse practitioner, a job she loved, but since the threats had come, she'd had to change how she went to work and even had to inform her supervisor.

"Work is good. I just...it's nothing."

"No, what is it?"

"It's really nothing. I'll just be very happy when things can go back to normal again."

"It will; have faith," Freddy said with a large smile.

"And that's why I love you, Becker, always the optimist."

"Never been called that, but I'll take the moniker."

Janie smiled and sweetly said, "Thanks again for being a good friend to Ryan."

"No thanks needed for that. This is what friends do for each other."

Janie gave him a nervous smile and went back to her seat next to Kaitlyn.

"A huge explosion just rocked the downtown area. We have reporters on their way to the scene of the incident, but preliminary reports are revealing exclusively to us that a popular downtown nightclub was the location of what is believed to be an act of terrorism. We will report any further findings as they occur," the radio broadcaster reported before going back to playing music.

"What was that?" Kaitlyn asked loudly from her seat.

Freddy looked over to her. Both she and Janie were standing up. "They said there was another explosion downtown at a nightclub. They believe it was another terror attack."

"When do you think this is going to end?" Janie asked.

"Honestly, I don't," Freddy said. "The principles that are driving the terrorists to do what they do are religious ideals. They're ready to die for what they believe in, no matter how ridiculous it is. The only real way to end it is to eradicate every last one of the scumbags. After that, nuke their goats, their homes, and even their children."

Kaitlyn gasped. "Frederick!"

"Sorry, not sorry. Those animals won't stop killing us. Ever! If they're not utterly annihilated, then they'll keep coming. If you kill them, but not their kids, then they'll come for us, too."

She knew his approach would work, but the thought of

killing children repulsed her. However, Janie seemed okay with the idea.

"Don't worry for them," Janie said. "They get to go be with a thousand virgins when they're martyred. Sorry if I seem callous, but my daddy was a war vet, and he talked like a sailor in front of us kids. I'm a lot like him."

"What's keeping Ryan?" Freddy asked Janie.

"I'll go check on him. He's probably lost. I have to help him everywhere he goes. He's totally helpless without me," she joked, leaving to go check on Ryan. No sooner than she reached the door, he came walking out of the house.

"Everything come out okay?" Janie asked.

"Yeah. Everything's fine. Why?" Ryan asked, a hurried look on his face.

"Just that you were gone a while. I was about to come pull you out," Janie replied as she took notice of his look.

"He must've heard the radio broadcast," Freddy said.

"Radio broadcast?" Ryan asked, his tone showing confusion.

"Yeah, there was another attack. Downtown this time," Freddy answered as he flipped the burgers again.

"Oh yeah. I can't believe those whackos are still on about *America, the great Satan.*"

"We were just talking about that. I don't think it's going to end until they've been erased off the face of the planet."

"I'll drink to that," Ryan said, raising a beer to Freddy.

Freddy grabbed his beer and they toasted to the eradication of Islamism.

NOVEMBER 10, 2014
DIVISION OF PAROLE, CHICAGO

FREDDY THOUGHT the day was going to be more of the usual: clock and log in, investigate, make an arrest, log and clock out, then go home. However, today wasn't going to go that way.

His bad day began when he discovered his service pistol was missing. Kaitlyn swore she never touched it. Both Michael and Kayleigh denied any knowledge of its absence. It was possible that he'd left everything at work, but he doubted it.

Everybody in the department stared at Agent Becker as he made his way to his office space. *What are they staring at?* he wondered. It was almost like something was wrong – terribly wrong – and he was the center of it all.

Largely distracted by his colleagues and Chicago's finest, he nearly failed to see the two officers standing just outside his office door. When he did, his heart sank. At first, he thought maybe they were taking notice that his pistol was missing from his hip. That didn't make sense, though. These officers and agents had been staring at him from the moment he walked in the door, so he dismissed that notion. Besides, it didn't make sense to have two officers at his door because his pistol was missing. *What, then? What could be wrong?* Maybe they weren't there for him. Maybe they were just standing in his way.

Freddy finally reached his office door. The two officers stepped aside and let him enter. He was relieved for a moment. He went to unlock the door, but the knob turned. It was unlocked. Nothing unusual, Ryan usually got to work first. *Did something happen to Ryan? What's going on here?*

He opened the door to find his supervisor, Captain Reyes, sitting at his desk. "Captain, what's going on?" Freddy asked, his tone showing his surprise.

"Agent Becker, just the man I was waiting for."

"Oh yeah?"

"I'll need you to surrender your badge."

"Ahh, you need what?" Freddy asked, his surprise turning to shock.

Reyes stood. "Stop the bullshit, Becker, and give me your badge."

"Captain, what's this about?"

"I'll explain after you surrender your badge," Reyes insisted.

Freddy saw Captain Reyes's eyes move toward the door. It

was a signal for the two men, who Freddy now knew were there as backup.

The two police officers stepped into the office as a show of force.

It was enough to tell Freddy that something was indeed terribly wrong. He took his badge from his belt and placed it on his own desk.

Captain Reyes picked it up, gave it a quick look, and sighed.

Freddy was unsure if it was a sigh of relief or concern.

"Agent Becker, you're being investigated for the murder of Hidalgo Dominguez."

"Who?" Freddy answered after a moment of silence. He was completely taken aback, being caught off guard by something so ludicrous.

"He's a local Latin Kings gangbanger."

"Captain, there's gotta be some kind of mistake here."

"You're gonna have to tell it to the judge, Becker."

"Captain Reyes, you've known me for years. You know I'm a lawman. I don't murder people." Freddy looked around and noticed Ryan was not present. "Where's Agent Pettigrew?"

"He's been relocated. That's all I can tell you."

Relocated? Nothing was making sense. Nothing.

The phone rang.

Captain Reyes answered.

All Freddy could do was watch and listen to Reyes's side of the conversation.

"This is Reyes. Yeah? That's disappointing news. Thank you, officer." Reyes hung up the phone.

Freddy waited and watched Reyes, his face displaying an intensity he didn't see often. "Captain?"

Reyes looked at the officers. "Cuff him!"

One of the officers went to grab Freddy, but he pulled away.

"Why are you cuffing me, Captain?" Freddy pleaded as the two officers tried to get his arms and place the cuffs on. Freddy wasn't having any of it, though, as he fought back. "Why are you doing this? Tell me!" he barked.

Confusion and fear gripped Freddy. He knew he hadn't killed anyone, but right now that didn't matter. He was being charged with it, and when that happened, you normally were cuffed.

Unable to get him under control, the three went to the ground in a violent scuffle, Freddy not allowing himself to go peacefully.

"I'm innocent. I've not done anything. Captain, you gotta believe me," Freddy wailed.

The brute force of the two officers was finally too much. They had Freddy pinned facedown to the floor.

The all-too-familiar sound of the handcuffs clicking hit Freddy's ears. But this time, these cuffs were on him.

Now secure, the officers patted him down, then brought him to his feet.

"That little display you just put on makes you look guiltier than ever," Reyes said as he walked closer to Freddy.

"The boy you say you didn't kill had an entire magazine emptied into him late Saturday night. The magazine was left at the scene and was covered with your prints. We only made the connection because of an anonymous tip. The judge signed off on a warrant to search your vehicle. We found what we were looking for – the murder weapon. Fitting that you're not wearing one now. As for the call I just received, your service pistol was found under your driver's seat. We believe the magazine with your fingerprints belongs to the Glock you used to kill that boy. We're going to be sending it to the lab for ballistics testing. I hope we're wrong, Becker."

Freddy's mind was twirling with both confusion and chaos. It was a setup – it had to be. But who?

8

DECEMBER 4, 2014

COOK COUNTY COURTHOUSE, CHICAGO

IT TOOK ONLY three short hours for the jury of six men and six women to reach a verdict on the murder of Hidalgo Dominguez.

As they made their way out to the jury box, Freddy sat in silence, his body tense with anxiety.

"Has the jury reached a decision?" Judge Schnoeker asked.

"Yes, we have, Your Honor," the head juror answered and surrendered the verdict to the bailiff, who turned and took it to Judge Schnoeker.

Schnoeker opened the folded paper and reviewed the verdict with a face that a master poker player would envy.

About to burst, Freddy cocked his head over his shoulder to see if Kaitlyn was there, but found she wasn't.

Almost frantic to find them in the crowd, he kept looking,

only to find one familiar face, and that was his father-in-law's, James Allen Browning.

James was a man of impeccable character. He believed Freddy was innocent with every fiber of his being.

The two made eye contact.

James gave Freddy a nod, but he knew it wasn't he who Freddy was looking for. He shrugged as a way to tell Freddy he didn't know where Kaitlyn and the kids were.

Disheartened, Freddy turned back to face Judge Schnoeker and his fate.

Schnoeker turned to the head juror and said, "How does the jury find the defendant?"

"We, the jury, find Frederick Douglas Becker guilty of first-degree murder."

Freddy got up from his seat and turned in James's direction. "Find my family. Let me know what's happened to them."

"Mr. Becker will return to his seat," Judge Schnoeker barked.

Freddy acknowledged and sat down.

Schnoeker collected himself and said, "Given the fact that Frederick Becker has a spotless record and has served this county for several years now, the court is showing leniency and sentencing him to life in prison with the possibility of parole in ten years."

The court immediately erupted into jeers and complaints.

"Order in the court!" Schnoeker yelled as he slammed his gavel down repeatedly.

The crowd didn't listen and only grew louder with complaints.

"Order in the court," Schnoeker yelled again. Still, they refused to silence themselves. "Bailiff, remove those men and women from my court!"

Cook County guards ran in to assist with the tumultuous crowd.

Several men in the crowd raced towards Freddy, with one penetrating the court's security. He cocked back and struck Freddy in the face with a tightly clenched fist.

Freddy took the punch and stood up from his seated position, ready to fight quite possibly for his life. Before he could do anything, several guards grabbed Freddy by the arms and escorted him to safety.

9

DECEMBER 5, 2014
COOK COUNTY JAIL, CHICAGO

FREDDY HAD BARELY SERVED a day in the Cook County Receiving Area before he found out he was soon to be transferred to Menard Correctional facility in Southern Illinois.

Since Freddy had arrested so many people, he found it hard to maintain a low profile in the Cook County system. No matter where he went within the jail, no matter what he did, he found himself looking over his shoulder. Jail time was hard by itself, but trying to survive in the big house with a background in law enforcement was worse than being a pedophile rapist. Freddy found that there was a pecking order in the prison system. Murderers were at the top. Way down, near the bottom, was where the rapists, pedophiles, and ex-cops belonged.

However, he did have friends, and they were the correctional officers. To them he was a saint and had earned their admiration and respect for killing a gangbanger whom they defined as nothing but a scourge on society.

Freddy sat in deep thought. His life in literally an instant had turned on a dime. He was now the one behind bars and the one who hoped to get parole someday. It was irony at its best.

Heavy footfalls from the hall outside his cell told Freddy a guard was coming.

The guard, a familiar and friendly face, emerged in front of the door. He unlocked it and tossed a jumpsuit at Freddy.

"What's this?" Freddy asked, his hands holding up the famous orange jumpsuit often popularized on television and in movies.

"Get dressed, Becker. The warden has arranged your transfer."

"Transfer?"

"You're going into protective custody. He's not sure why you weren't given it from the start. It doesn't matter now. It's been rectified. Get dressed. You're transferring."

FREDDY DIDN'T KNOW if he should be excited about protective custody or not, as it posed its own risks. He hoped the place was filled with ex-law enforcement and informants, as it was the only way he would be able to let his guard down.

On the bus, Freddy found himself sitting next to three other inmates, each handcuffed at the wrists with a waist chain that connected the two. And to ensure they could not run, each was also adorned with ankle shackles.

Sitting in the back with unencumbered views of the inmates were two correctional officers armed with service pistols and shotguns.

The bus rumbled to a start and lurched forward towards the gate. In no time they'd departed the massive gates and were on the highway headed south.

Freddy had the opportunity to be seated near a window. His gaze fixed on the sights of buildings, trees and people as they passed. So many were going about their lives while his had essentially ended.

An early winter storm had blanketed the ground with snow, but typical Chicago weather proved, if anything, to be consistent; as the sun appeared, the temperatures rose, easily melting the fresh powder.

The skies were clear and the traffic was bustling. The guards revealed to Freddy and the others that they were being transferred to a protective custody unit at Pontiac Correctional Facility. It was a maximum-security facility.

Freddy hoped that in time, he'd make the cut for a medium-confinement prison, but he was still very early on in the system. It would take some time to develop a rapport with the *powers that be* for such a transfer. For now, Pontiac had to suffice.

The bus was barely out of Chicago when the driver began cursing unintelligibly.

Freddy couldn't hear exactly what he was saying, but he could feel the bus slow as if it had stalled.

The sounds of squealing brakes, tires, and traffic crashes filled the air.

Everyone on the bus peered out to see the confusing display of cars and trucks slamming into each other.

Then without notice, their bus was hit.

Freddy's entire body was jolted by the impact of a dump truck as it collided with the side of the armored bus. The impact was jarring, to say the least, but was nothing compared to the train that was pushing its way down the track. Freddy looked back to get the attention of the two guards who were safely secured behind the security fence in the back of the bus.

The force from the dump truck pushed the bus onto the train tracks, where they came to a stop.

Everyone looked around with wide eyes. No one knew what had happened, but it appeared that not only the bus, but many of the vehicles around them had also lost power.

"Get it moving," a guard barked to the driver.

"I'm trying," he yelled. "It won't start." The driver tried fervently to ignite the engine.

"There's a train coming; get this thing started!" the guard roared, a panicked look on his face.

Freddy and the other inmates craned their heads in the direction of the oncoming train.

"Come on," Freddy bellowed.

"It won't start!" the driver shouted back.

The first guard slapped the other on the shoulder and pointed to the western sky.

Freddy caught this and swiveled his head in the direction the guard was pointing, to see a huge orange light about the size of the sun. Confused by what he was seeing, Freddy asked, "What is that?"

With everyone but the driver focused on the peculiar light in the sky, they weren't paying attention to the pressing threat at the moment, the train that was heading right for them.

Fearful, the inmates tried to leave their seats, and even the driver saw the writing on the wall. There was no getting the bus started, so he'd best evacuate now. He unbuckled and went for the door, but it wouldn't budge. The impact from the dump truck had damaged it, making it inoperable.

The guards too attempted to leave but found the locks unresponsive.

The driver grabbed a fire extinguisher and used it like a hammer. He repeatedly slammed it against the door until it broke loose. But it was too late.

Freddy tried to move, but like the other inmates, he was chained to the floor of the bus. There wasn't anything he could do but pray for a miracle.

With incredible force, the train slammed into the side of the bus.

Screams and cries came from all on board.

Freddy's head smacked against the side of the bus. He tried to shake it off, but the blunt-force impact was too much.

Just before he fell unconscious, he heard the others wailing in fear and pain as well as the tortured screech of metal.

The last image he saw in his mind's eye was Kaitlyn.

Pettigrew Residence, Chicago

"Hello?" Janie said to her mom on the now dead phone. "Mom, are you there?" She pulled the phone away from her face and stared at it oddly, hoping to see the call was active. She gazed down at the blackened screen.

Nothing.

"Honey? My phone just went dead," she called out to Ryan.

"Here, use mine," Ryan said, handing his phone to Janie. She pushed the home button, but nothing happened. "Wait, this is weird."

"What's wrong?" Ryan asked.

"Your phone is dead too," Janie said. "Did you remember to charge yours? It's dead."

"That's weird. It was fully charged a moment ago," he said, plucking the phone from her hand. He attempted to turn it on, but nothing happened. "What the hell?"

"I don't know," Janie said in frustration. "My mom needs my help, and now I can't reach her."

Still trying to get his phone to turn on, Ryan said, "I don't know either. Just plug it in and help me unpack these boxes." He was referring to the household goods they still had in boxes from their recent move.

The city paid for Ryan's relocation to his current residence. The situation that got him and his family relocated was a sensitive topic, and Ryan refused to talk about it with Janie. In truth, Ryan refused to tell her the truth regarding their relocation. He preferred the cover story – that the threats on his family's life merited the move.

Janie felt a sudden draft.

"Brrr," she said, hugging herself. "It got chilly in here." Janie went for the thermostat and noticed the screen display was dark and not working. "Hon, the thermostat thingy isn't working either," she said, tapping the fixture as if to wake it up.

Ryan stopped unpacking and walked over to Janie. He tapped the screen, believing he could fix it under pressure of human influence. Nothing. He stood still and put his finger up. Janie recognized his intention. He wanted her to be quiet while he listened to the air flow.

"Do you hear that?"

"I don't hear anything," she answered.

"Exactly. I think the power went out in the neighborhood."

Janie went to the refrigerator and opened the door. "Yep, power's out," she said. "Better run to the store and buy some ice for the cooler."

Ryan agreed. He kissed her on the cheek and grabbed the keys from the kitchen counter. "Be right back." As he made his way to the carport, he saw several neighbors trying to start their vehicles. He found it quite odd.

He pressed the keyless entry on the fob, but the car didn't respond. He dismissed the issue after a few more times, then used the hard key to open the door. He hopped in the driver's seat, put the keys in the ignition and turned, to find it wouldn't start. "What's going on here?" he asked himself. He tried again. Not even the lights of their 2010 Chevrolet Equinox turned on. It was as if the battery was completely dead. He stepped out of the car and hollered over the fence at one of his neighbors, "Hey, Tom, what's going on with the power and vehicles? Why aren't they starting?"

"Yeah, I don't know, Ryan. It's like everything electronic has quit working."

"Everything electronic?"

"Yeah, phones, cars, trucks, appliances, the lights in my house – everything that runs off electricity is out," Tom said.

"I wonder what would cause such a thing," Ryan asked, his hands on his hips as he stared at Tom, hoping he'd give him an answer to the strange occurrence.

"My sister-in-law always said something like this would happen. I figured her for crazy. She doesn't read anything but those post-apocalyptic books. They've got her mind all frazzled."

"Something like this?" Ryan asked.

"Eh, she's nuttier than a squirrel turd. She's one of them prepper types. She has everything she owns in some kind of electromagnetic-proof containers."

"You're talking about an EMP?"

"Yeah, that's it," Tom replied as a grin appeared on his face.

Ryan didn't need to hear anything more. He dropped his car keys on the ground and went into the house, shut the door, and bolted it.

Outskirts of Chicago

Freddy woke. He sat up, blinking repeatedly, to find he was several yards from the intersection where the train had collided with the bus.

A warm and steady stream of blood coursed down his forehead, dripping onto the pavement. He scanned the area from left to right. It looked like a war zone. Debris and bodies were everywhere. Not ten feet from his position, the inmate who sat next to him had apparently been disemboweled by the train, giving credence to the fact that Freddy was incredibly fortunate to still be breathing. Feet further, the driver's body lay, his chest visibly crushed.

An inmate and one of the correctional officers were yards away to his right. They moaned and called out for help, but nobody seemed attentive to their screams.

Freddy pulled himself to a utility pole and leaned up against it. What shocked him was his ability to even do that. This gave him hope and some proof that he was unscathed.

Carnage surrounded him, but not all was from the train crash. Behind him on the road leading to the train tracks were wrecked cars. What struck him as odd was the absence of police or firefighters. Not even the familiar wail of a siren. The only thing that filled the air and his ears were the screams of the injured. He had no answer for what was happening, but whatever it was, he thought it had something to do with the same strange glowing anomaly in the southwestern sky.

Freddy Becker's world had changed again. Not for the better, either. He was still trying to collect all the details. He thought his transport bus had been the lone recipient of an out-of-the-ordinary incident, but the details he was processing about his environment told a different story.

A few feet from him, he saw a man arguing with his cell phone. Feet from that man, he heard another say that he had no service. Yet another he heard complain that her phone wouldn't even turn on. With the new information at hand, Freddy turned his sights toward the technological aspect.

As his mind tried to come to grips with what had happened, screams came from south of his position. Freddy looked and saw a man pointing upward.

"Take cover!" the man yelled.

Freddy shifted his eyes up to see what looked like a plane falling from the sky. But how could that be? He blinked several times just to make sure he wasn't seeing things; then he confirmed it was a plane and it was headed straight for them. There wasn't much time. He scurried to the correctional officer who had since died, took the keys from his duty belt, unlocked the restraints on his wrists and ankles, and took off at a sprint, hurdling debris and bodies.

He quickly glanced up to see the plane was drawing closer. He didn't have much time; he needed to take cover somewhere.

Ahead he saw a building where he hoped he'd be able to take refuge, but it was too late.

With a terrifying boom and earth-shattering force, the plane impacted the ground.

The concussion toppled Freddy. He slammed into the hard ground, his face skidding off the pavement. Still able to react, he quickly crawled to a large oak tree and got behind it.

A subsequent explosion rocked the area and rained down countless pieces of debris.

Freddy could feel the heat from the explosion rush past him, and it took with it all the breathable air. He could not stay where he was, it was too dangerous, and now everything around him was on fire.

He stood up once more and ran, jumping over an occasional screaming and injured pedestrian. The victims of the plane crash were on fire, and their corpses were rapidly being consumed by the inferno.

It was at that moment that he realized he had a chance and a choice to make. *Do I stay, or do I go?* The chaos that controlled the moment tipped the scale in the direction of fleeing, but that would make him a fugitive on top of being a felon. He knew what he was, and he wasn't either of those.

What do I do? he thought.

Freddy felt like he had all the time in the world to think it over and, at the same time, no time at all. As if he were frozen in time. Stuck in the moment that could liberate him from the binds of his prison, he sat still and tried to quiet his mind.

Kaitlyn, Michael, and Kayleigh popped into his mind. They had to be saved. Nothing else mattered. Not the guards, not the inmates, not the loss of technology – nothing.

Freddy made his decision, or he thought he did. For a moment, he considered the fact that he had been framed for the murder of Hidalgo Dominguez, a thug he had never even heard of. *Do I bring justice to my name? Do I uncover the truth?* Once again, Freddy found himself at a standstill. He looked out across the landscape. Nothing had changed. There were no emergency vehicles. No law enforcement. There was nothing but disorder and confusion. The second revelation that he was utterly alone hit him like a ton of bricks. Then he knew his decision was a clear one. A finality. *I run.*

Freddy ran north toward Chicago's city limits. Everywhere he looked, it was the same. Traffic crashes and no help to be heard of. Even the few times he saw a police officer, he noticed that they were doing their own thing. He was beginning to see the truth of it all. That he had to deal with a new way of life, as nothing was making any sense.

Freddy heard some gunshots. He turned his attention toward them. The police were being attacked by random citizens. Stores were being looted. People were being robbed on the streets at gunpoint. In the moment, crime prevailed. Violence had supreme reign. There was nobody to stop it.

That was the moment Freddy had his first run-in with the new reality. He felt a sudden impact to the back of his head.

He fell to the ground, dazed and confused. He rolled over to see a blurry-faced person searching Freddy's body up and down. It took a moment for Freddy to realize he was being mugged. It didn't matter, though. He had been mid-transfer when the crisis hit. He had no possessions, only the orange jumpsuit on his back.

Then his senses finally returned. Freddy reached out and grabbed the hand of the man who had attacked him. The man tried to strike back, but Freddy parried the strike and caught the man's arm. Since Freddy was on his back, his options were limited. He pulled the man's arm out straight and bent the wrist to configure an armbar technique. Freddy locked it out as tight as he could. He even used his legs to help strengthen the joint lock.

Off to the side Freddy saw a brick, which had been the perpetrator's weapon to attack him. Freddy had to make another decision. He either had to maintain the joint lock or let go so he could grab the brick and use it as a weapon.

There's no law and order. There're no emergency response vehicles, he thought to himself quickly.

It was against his better judgment, but Freddy weighed the fact that the man might very well kill him, so it was best to kill him instead. Freddy let go of the man's wrist.

The man immediately went for Freddy's throat; he locked his fat fingers and began to squeeze.

The brick was just out of reach, Freddy's fingers barely touching it.

The man's grip tightened on Freddy's neck, making it

hard to breathe. Darkness began to overtake his vision, but he refused to give up.

With all his might, Freddy stretched. He grabbed the brick and swung it, striking the side of the man's head.

The attacker went limp, and Freddy's eyesight was restored.

For a second Freddy contemplated smashing the brick against the man's head until he was dead, but he figured the immediate threat was over, so that was all that mattered. He shoved the man off him and got to his feet. "What a day," he grunted.

Not wasting another second, he started out on his trek again. His priority was to get as far away from the train crash site as possible.

With each step he took, he formulated a plan. If he had the opportunity to be free, he would do all he could to clear his name. It might be an impossible task, as from all appearances the shit had hit the fan. One thing he needed to do was figure out what exactly had happened. Was it a local thing, or was this something much larger? He didn't know, but he was determined to find out.

He passed the storefront of a small mom-and-pop business when he caught the reflection of himself and noticed the orange jumpsuit. He stood for a moment and stared at himself. It was hard to recognize himself in such garb, yet here he was.

Determination filled him to his core. He would clear his

name, he would regain his life and his family; but before he could do anything, he'd have to find a change of clothes.

Cook County Jail, Chicago

Chaos! That's the only word that could describe what was occurring. When the lights went out, with it went the ability to control the masses of inmates.

Antonio saw the flashlights moving around in the control center. It was pitch black everywhere else, except for the control center. If those flashlights were flames, then the inmates were the moths. Inmates from both units piled against the control center windows. Antonio could hear the inmates striking the glass with their fists, but he knew it was to no avail.

The sound of a shotgun suddenly erupted from the darkness behind where Antonio was standing. The inmates grew silent for just a moment as they all turned to face in the direction of the flash.

The inmates must have control of the armory, Antonio thought. He was worried enough that he might get shanked by an opposing gang member, but with the lights out, there seemed to be solidarity between them.

Unexpectedly, the two control center guards shined their flashlights in the direction of the shotgun blast.

It was an inmate, and he had a shotgun, but what made it look like a scene from a horror movie was the inmate was covered in blood.

For Antonio, all he wanted was to survive the blackout and subsequent riot. He didn't know what had caused the blackout or what was going on, but he thought it was strange SORT (Special Operations Response Team) hadn't showed up yet. SORT was an elite trained group that managed riots and other scenarios too dangerous for the average guard.

Without information and assuming all that had occurred was a simple power outage, Antonio planned on riding this out with hopes he'd make it.

After a while, the two guards could be seen talking. It was believed they were talking about leaving the control room and making a run for it. The control center was never left unattended. Never! It was a mandatory position, so when they made their way to the exit that would come out between the two key-locked gates, the inmates knew they would have only one chance at escape. The guards had keys on them. Keys that could open the gates.

The inmate with the shotgun had made his way to the gate nearest the guards. The correctional officers didn't know he was lying in wait. He had blended in with the inmates by this time and was invisible in the near impenetrable darkness. Had the correctional officers turned their flashlights off, they would have disappeared, as well.

Antonio watched as the two guards stood at the door with their flashlights on. They opened the door, which pulled inward, and began to make a run for it. That was when another shotgun blast went off. A flashlight dropped to the ground. Inmates started cheering. The energy in the cellblock rose substantially. There were some more arguments. Another shotgun blast. Some yells. Some cheers. Then a third shotgun blast. Another flashlight hit the floor. Antonio stood in the crowd of inmates and tried to piece together what was happening. The best he figured was that both guards were now dead or dying.

The room began to clear out. It was obvious by this point that the gate had been unlocked and the inmates were fleeing the cellblocks. Antonio followed the crowd. Now with nothing to lose, he dreamed of freedom for a moment. But then there was an interruption in his imaginations of blue skies and open borders. It was the thought of exacting his revenge on Agent Freddy Becker. The man who didn't give him a chance. The man who took him from a dying mother and pillar of the community. But he'd have to be careful, else-wise he might get picked up and returned to prison.

Antonio followed the trail of inmates through the dark corridors until the band came to a complete stop. The energy level spiked again. Inmates could be heard yelling and swearing. There was another shotgun blast. Then the line began to move again. Step by step, Antonio made his way closer and closer to freedom. It wasn't long before he tripped over something. It was a body. He didn't stop his advancement toward freedom; he walked on the dead person and kept going. Suddenly, there was a flood of light streaming into the building. It was the outside. Finally, they were outside.

They were met by a twenty-foot sandstone wall and a sally port gate connected to a tower where there was usually a guard with a rifle positioned. It was vacant, and the lower guard tower door was open, as was the sally port gate. Whoever was assigned to it had fled the premises. Antonio followed the crowd and did the same.

Once he reached the outside perimeter, it was apparent that something was terribly wrong. Vehicles filled the street, north to south, as far as his eyes could see. None of them were moving. In fact, the driver of each vehicle and, in most cases, the passengers were standing outside their respective car or truck – all of them surprised to see the inmates pouring out of the prison. Screams filled the air as inmate after inmate ran to vehicles and attacked the owners in a futile attempt to carjack them.

Pew, pew, pew.

Antonio turned his head toward the sound of a pistol as it discharged its projectiles. An inmate fell to the ground. The man with the gun was a free citizen trying to defend his family from an escaped convict. His victory over the inmate was short-lived. Other inmates responded to the gunshots. The man emptied his clip toward the deluge of escapees. Some fell, but eventually, they overcame him. The man was killed there, in front of his wife and small children. The man's death was violent and senseless. The woman was attacked, too. She was last seen alive kneeling beside her collapsed husband. The children were left behind as orphans – forced into a life without parents in a frenzied new world.

Antonio stood motionless. Still trying to take in what was happening, he felt like a fish out of water.

Pettigrew Residence, Chicago

Ryan stood just inside the house, behind the bolted door. He remained skeptical about the EMP idea. He headed to the basement. Looking at the breakers, he failed to uncover any other reason for the power outage. That was when Janie followed him back outside. Much of the neighborhood was standing outside in their quiet up-scale community. Each of them was confused about what had happened.

Ryan grabbed his cell phone, but it was still an empty blacked-out screen. It just wouldn't turn on. Janie tried turning hers on again. Nothing. It wasn't just them. The more the neighbors talked, the more it became apparent that an EMP might have actually happened. Nobody's phone was working. One neighbor complained that his battery-operated electronics weren't working, either.

Janie ran back inside the house and grabbed her fully charged laptop. Nothing. She then ran to the kitchen, hoping to grab the emergency flashlight from the junk drawer. It wasn't there. Then it dawned on her that she had packed it up. She and Ryan had spent the last several hours unpacking from their big move to the new home. Remembering that she'd packed the flashlight into a box labeled "JUNK DRAW-ERS," she headed to the kitchen. She dug through the box and found it. The flashlight worked!

What else is not working? she thought, running to more electronic items. Everything that required electrical power failed. Some battery-operated devices still worked as long as they didn't have any sophisticated components like microchips and/or motherboards. When her investigation was complete, she went back outside.

Ryan was standing next to a neighbor, and they were already in the middle of a conversation.

"Think about it," the neighbor said. "No power. No electronics. Life as we know it is gone. Surely the Lord is coming back and this world is going to hell."

Ryan gave it some thought. He wasn't a religious man, but he was expecting a little more *flare* if Jesus was coming back.

"The Bible says that the earth will be destroyed by fire next time," the neighbor said.

Ryan rubbed his face, frustrated about everything that was happening. He turned to face Janie. "Where'd you go?"

"I went to check on our electronics."

"And?"

"And nothing's working. Not even my laptop. It had a full battery before the power went out."

The neighbor walked away.

"What were you guys talking about?" Janie asked Ryan.

"He thinks the Lord's coming back, and something about an EMP, but I think we were hit by a CME."

"A CME?"

"A coronal mass ejection. I was talking about this at work a couple of weeks back. I saw a special on it, too. It makes perfect sense."

"Should we be concerned?"

"I think so. It could take weeks, upward of months, to get our power back."

"What do we do until then?"

"I would say we should go stay with your dad in Kentucky, but we have no way of getting there."

"What do you mean? We can take the car."

"There's not a car in the area that's functioning. They're all dead."

"I don't know. We can't call him or get to him, anyway."

"You're right," Ryan answered, storming off into the house. "You need to come inside."

Instead, Janie stood there, trying to take in the enormity of what was happening. That was when they heard the roar. Janie looked up and saw a low-flying airplane. They weren't that far from O'Hare International Airport. The planes were never this low, though. It was barely a hundred feet over the treetops.

"Whoa," the neighbors yelled.

The plane disappeared behind the building; then an explosion could be heard. The ground rumbled.

Janie ran inside.

Ryan was in the garage, and the hood of his Equinox was lifted. Ryan was grabbing the back of his head, refusing to believe.

"Ryan," she called.

"Yeah?"

"Did you hear that?"

"Yeah, what was it?"

"It was an airplane. I think it crashed."

Something clicked in Ryan's mind. It was beginning to make sense. Those neighbors weren't so crazy after all. "It's true!" Ryan said, ignoring Janie.

"Ryan, people are dead!"

Realizing the severity of it all, he replied, "Janie, I'm afraid we'll all be dead if we don't take defensive measures now."

10

DECEMBER 6, 2014
CHICAGO

ALL NIGHT long Freddy listened to the sounds of gunfire and cries for help as predator and prey collided in the darkness. He would have normally tried to navigate the night, but his gut told him it was too dangerous, and without a weapon he felt useless.

He had always been a man who thrived on information. When the kids got sick, he didn't feel secure until he knew what the diagnosis was; only then could he find a solution. This was no different. He knew something had happened, but what and how widespread? He wouldn't feel right until he knew the parameters and rules of this new world.

His mind was cluttered with thoughts, but the one thing that kept coming back over and over was his family. He didn't have the luxury of time to sit around and contemplate what had happened, or the politics of it all. All he needed to focus on was how he'd navigate this new landscape without getting killed.

Finding his purpose, he pulled himself together and left for home and his family.

IT WAS NEARLY noon and Freddy was making good time. He had one city block to maneuver before reaching his neighborhood. He had done well, but as a stroke of bad luck would have it, a man jumped out of the alleyway in his final stretch for home. He recognized the man. He had seen him a hundred times over. It was the beggar. The man he'd ignored for countless trips to work and back. Freddy remembered him clearly. He was a veteran, or at least that was what his handwritten sign said. Emblazoned in black marker, it read, *VETERAN WILL WORK FOR FOOD.*

This run-in was different. He wasn't holding a sign – he was holding a switchblade knife. It was cliché, for sure.

"What is this?" Freddy asked.

"I remember you," the homeless man said.

"I don't want any trouble. I'm just trying to make it home to my wife and children."

"Well, the streets are my home, and my family gave up on me years ago."

"Sorry to hear that," Freddy replied in a mocking tone.

"You think you're better than me, don't you?"

"As a matter of fact...I do." Just beyond the man lay

several bodies; it was clear to Freddy they were freshly deceased, as the blood hadn't had time to coagulate. One of the bodies, a woman in her thirties, had dropped her purse during a struggle. From where he was standing, he could clearly see a small hand-sized semiautomatic pistol lying within the contents of the woman's purse. Finally, his investigative background was coming in handy in a situation outside of law enforcement.

He didn't hesitate because hesitation could literally cost him his life. He leaped forward toward the dead woman's purse, which surprised the man, who went for him. Freddy's quick thinking and action worked. He reached the pistol, released the safety with his thumb, and turned towards the man, who was advancing.

The tables had turned, and the man knew it as his face turned from anger to fear.

Freddy squeezed the trigger. A round roared from the muzzle and struck the man in the chest. Not satisfied with one hit, Freddy again squeezed the trigger and unleashed a second round; this too found its home in the man's chest.

The man stumbled and fell onto him.

Disgusted, Freddy tossed him off and got to his feet right away.

Still clinging to the knife and still very much alive, the man lay now in a pool of his own blood.

"I'm not only better than you, I'm quicker," Freddy sneered. He raised the pistol and put one final round in the man's face.

That kill was legal, Freddy thought, grabbing the knife and putting the blade back in. He put the pistol in his right pocket and the knife in his left. After realizing he was safe, he let out a thankful sigh, then set off to finish the final stretch.

ADRENALINE and a strong will to protect his family was all Freddy was operating on. He reached his home, ran to the back, and pulled the screen door open, only to find the main door locked.

Praying they were home, he started banging.

Nothing.

Fearing for his family's safety, he ran to the front door, to find that screen door was off its hinges. Terror gripped him as he feared the worst. He gave the door a push. It burst open, toppling him to the floor. He quickly hopped to his feet, to discover the house was trashed. Pieces of drywall and wood littered the floor. It looked like his home had been picked clean from the inside out.

"Kaitlyn?" he cried out.

No answer.

"Michael, Kayleigh?" he yelled.

Still no answer.

He bolted from the living room and into the kitchen.

Nothing but more damage and signs that someone had tried to board up the windows.

His heart raced. He was on the verge of a panic attack.

"Kaitlyn...Michael...Kayleigh!" he howled as he sprinted from the kitchen to the children's bedrooms. He threw open the closets.

Nothing.

He ran to the master bedroom.

Nothing but debris and more signs that the house had been ransacked.

With the entire house searched and no closer to knowing where they were, he crumpled to the ground and sobbed. He'd been through so much in such a short period of time that it was beginning to wear on him. He put his head in his hands and tried to calm himself. He knew he couldn't help them if he was in a state of frenzy. "Where could you be? Where?" he asked out loud, but nothing came. For the first time in Freddy's memory, he had no playbook to guide him. There were no instructions, no laws, and no guidance. Nothing had prepared him for this. Life was no longer black and white.

A name popped in his head, *James*. His eyes widened. Maybe Kaitlyn had taken the kids there; that made sense. With all the chaos, she'd go to her dad's house, he just knew it. He only lived a few blocks away, so it was a short and easy trip. However, he wasn't leaving without some real firepower. In the basement he had a safe where he'd find what he needed.

Freddy picked himself up off the floor and went downstairs, only to find James lying on his side, with a pool of blood under his head. "Dad?" Freddy cried out. He ran to him and dropped to his knees. "No," he exclaimed as he rolled him over and placed his fingers on his carotid artery, hoping to find a pulse.

He felt the subtle throb of his heartbeat and breathed a sigh of relief. James was alive, but he was not in good shape.

Propping him up, Freddy asked, "Dad? Can you hear me?"

James's eyes opened.

"Thank God! I thought I lost you."

"I'm tougher than that, boy."

"Where's Kaitlyn?"

"When I saw the power go out, I didn't think nothing of it. But when the battery-operated thingamajigs stopped working, I knew something was terribly wrong. I went outside to talk to the neighbors. They were all speculating all sorts of crazy things, Armageddon, you name it. When I saw the plane falling, I knew it was something really awful, so..."

"Dad, focus, where is she?"

"I-I don't remember," he said, grabbing the sore spot on his head. "I remember Katy and the kids were scared...I started hearing gunshots in the neighborhood. Then, after that, I-I heard someone knocking on the door."

"Who was it, Dad? Can you remember?"

"It was an unfamiliar voice. A Hispanic man, I do remember that. He said he had news about you."

"What happened? Did he take Katy and the kids?"

"I don't know. I can't remember."

Frustrated, Freddy barked, "I need you to remember."

"I'm sorry, I don't. I, um," James replied. "Have you looked everywhere?"

"I've searched the house. They're not here."

"Fritz, how is it you're here?"

Freddy sighed. "It happened when they were transferring me to a protective custody unit."

"So you escaped?"

The word made Freddy cringe.

James always had a way to say things – directly. It was the most proficient way to communicate. It got worse with age. James believed that time worked against every man, so why waste your time tiptoeing around with words?

"I wouldn't call it an *escape*," Freddy replied, rubbing his face.

"Then what would you call it?"

"It doesn't matter. We need to find Kaitlyn and the kids."

"But what's happened? What's going on?"

"I think we've been hit by an EMP. I remember the transfer bus suddenly stopped operating. Then a train hit us, and I woke up surrounded by dead bodies and debris. Then there was the airplane. It might have been the one you saw, I don't know. It crashed and exploded not too far from me. I barely survived. I know you don't like the idea of me being an *escaped convict*, but I have to find Katy and the kids. Then I need to clear my name."

"No, Fritz, you just need to find Katy and the kids. That's it."

The comment shocked Freddy. Wasn't his father-in-law interested in him clearing his name?

James's eyes widened.

"That look, you remember something. What is it?"

"Some gangbangers took them."

Not needing to hear another word, Freddy stood up and headed to the safe, which was heavily damaged from an unsuccessful attempt to gain access.

"I don't remember any of that," James said, referring to the safe.

Freddy liked his gadgets, but when it came to his safety, he always went with tried and true. Instead of a high-tech biometric safe, he had one with an old dial.

He rotated the dial back and forth, and with a hard turn on the lever, the dead bolts released. He pulled hard on the heavy door to reveal his small arsenal. "Thank God for the Second Amendment." He grabbed his AR-15 and held it warmly in his grip, appreciative of his black rifle. Like the safe, he also kept his weapons simple, the rifle didn't have rails for optics or any other fancy gadgets. It was a standard-issue-looking rifle. He reached in again and pulled out several fully loaded thirty-round magazines. He inserted one in the magazine well, pulled back on the charging handle, then slapped the bolt release, which loaded a round into the chamber.

"What's the plan, Fritz?"

Freddy reached back into the safe and removed an M4

carbine. He handed it to James and said, "I'm going to start with Tony De LaRosa."

Undisclosed Location, Chicago

"Yo, Estevan, this place is drying up, man. We can't be staying here anymore," a young Hispanic man in his twenties said as he entered a darkened room with cracks of light shining through blanketed windows. He dumped the contents of a backpack full of canned goods onto a table in the middle of the front room.

The man named Estevan stood up from where he was sitting on the La-Z-Boy and walked over to the table. "This is all, Ricco? This is all you can find?"

Three other men who were sitting on a couch stood up to take their turn at inspecting the goods. With five men now standing around the table, the sounds of muffled screams could be heard from one of the back rooms. Estevan looked up at Ricco. "Go make yourself useful. You've got babysitting duty now."

Ricco gave Estevan a dirty look, then looked at the other three men, who were obviously backing up Estevan's instructions. They peered back at Ricco, refusing to be intimidated by a single man. The numbers were clearly in their favor.

Ricco left the room and followed the sounds of the woman's muffled screams.

KAITLYN'S MOUTH was tightly bound with duct tape and a dirty sock shoved into it. She was lying flat on her back, with her arms raised over her head and bound tightly by duct tape to a metal headboard. For her feet, rope was used, each ankle tied to the footboard. Her eyes were left uncovered so she could witness the horrors that were happening to her.

When Ricco came in, her nerves subsided. He was the only one who hadn't yet violated her. She could feel the bruises on her face each time she frowned or tried crying out. Her blood pressure would rise with each scream, putting the pain of the occasion to the front of her memory. Michael and Kayleigh were no longer with her. It was this that pained her the most.

"Estevan sent me to take over watch," Ricco said to Carlos.

"Have fun. She's extra feisty today," Carlos replied as he left.

"You wanna quit screaming, yeah?" Ricco said to Kaitlyn. "You don't know who you're dealing with here. These men will kill you and not lose a wink of sleep."

All Kaitlyn could do was try to speak to Ricco, but she knew he wouldn't understand a single syllable considering her mouth was bound and stuffed with a sock.

"I don't know why you do that," he said in frustration. "You know I can't understand you."

Kaitlyn was gambling on Ricco being the compassionate member of the gang. With a stroke of luck, she hoped she could at least get him to remove the gag so that she could be heard. She needed a chance – a chance to manipulate him into sharing the location of her children or, better yet, untying her. It was a long shot and she knew it, but it was worth a try.

She mumbled again, but this time, she made sure Ricco looked into her eyes. It was important that she let him see her eyes. Perhaps she could touch his sense of humanity.

It worked.

Ricco looked over his shoulder then went to the hallway and peeked out to ensure nobody was coming.

Kaitlyn feared for herself. She'd seen this several times before. Her "watchers" would look out the door, close it, then have their way with her. There were no rules against it except that she remain alive.

Ricco closed the door, knowing the others wouldn't interrupt him, thinking he was having some *alone time*, then turned to face Kaitlyn. "Listen, lady. I don't know you. I don't even know this man we're helping. All I know is that I'm not okay with what's been happening here. My mama raised me better. I'm only here because I'm trying to survive. I recommend you do the same thing. Try to survive. You're not going to if you try anything stupid. Now, listen to me carefully. Nod your head yes or no. If I take that gag off, do you promise not to yell?"

Kaitlyn nodded.

"Okay, do you promise not to do anything that would jeopardize our safety?"

Again, she nodded.

Ricco pulled a pocketknife from his pants.

Kaitlyn recoiled at first, then realized there was nothing she could do, so relented.

He cut the tape from her lips and pulled the saliva-soaked sock from her mouth. She didn't hesitate in pleading her case. "I need to know where my kids are. Please tell me that my kids are safe, and no harm has come to them."

"Keep your voice down," Ricco reminded her. "Your kids are in another room. They were alive when I left to go do some looting a couple of hours ago."

"But are they alive now? I need to know. Please, will you release me? I won't say a thing. I swear to God I won't say a thing. Just let me go – I just want to check on my kids. Please let me go."

Ricco had to cover her mouth with his hands. If the others in the front room heard a woman's voice and caught him talking to her, they might kill him. "You have to be quiet, or I'll put the gag back in."

She grew quiet.

"I'm going to remove my hands. You promise to keep it quiet?"

She nodded.

He took his hands from her mouth and again stated, "Keep it quiet."

"Please let me go," she whispered.

"I can't. They'll kill us both."

"Then let my kids go."

"What you're asking..."

"Then just check on my kids and promise me they're okay."

Ricco nodded his head. "I can do that," he said, grabbing the roll of tape that was on the stand by the bed and shoving the nasty sock back into her mouth. He rewrapped her head and hid the old tape that he'd cut off in his pocket. He promptly left the room, deliberately keeping the door ajar, looked up and saw Carlos standing in the hallway, leaning against the door that led to the front room.

Carlos smirked.

Ricco returned the gesture with a nod then moved to the next room to check on the children. He opened the door to find them secured together, back-to-back, with both duct tape and rope. Their mouths were also silenced with socks and tape. Content with the state he found them in, he returned to Kaitlyn, closing the door behind him.

"They're okay," he assured her.

She sighed. Tears followed.

"Now are you going to calm down?" he asked.

She nodded. Tears continued to flow.

Ricco hated what was happening. This wasn't him. Abusing women and torturing children wasn't what defined him, but what could he do?

The two stared at each other, both longing to be free.

Advocate Trinity Hospital, South Side Chicago

Antonio was beyond frustrated. The hospital staff were aggressively running around trying to keep their patients alive. When the electricity went out, there was immediate mass hysteria. Much of the hospital staff left their jobs to return home. Others, mainly the single staff and those with no children to care for, stayed behind to assist with the heavy workload. He couldn't seem to get the attention of any staff members but did manage to find his way up the stairs to the area where his mother had been kept.

Upon arrival, he was disheartened to discover his mother was no longer there. The passersby continued their hustle and bustle, only to be grabbed here and there by Antonio. Nobody seemed to have the answers. All he needed to know was where his mom's body had been taken. One nurse knew his mother and was able to point him in the right direction. "When nobody claimed your mother's body, she was moved to refrigeration. Unless she was taken to the morgue, that's probably where you're going to find her."

Antonio couldn't say thank you enough. He left in a hurry to find his mom. He followed the signs and made his way to the refrigerator, where they kept deceased patients until the morgue took possession. There were a few toe-tags for him to read, so to save time, he simply started pulling the covered cloths off the bodies of the deceased until they were all revealed. Nothing. His mother wasn't here.

He looked around for a person, hoping to find another

employee who would help, but the area was clear of assistance. Antonio was on his own. To make matters worse, the ensuing chaos in the city streets made traveling difficult. He would have to rely on his street-savvy skills to make it home, and even that might not be the safest place to go. As he was leaving the refrigerator, he saw a clipboard hanging on the wall. He stopped everything and ran around behind the desk to where it hung and took it off the wall. It was a transfer log.

Thank God!

The log showed that she had been moved to the city morgue. He had no idea where it was located. Antonio collapsed beneath his own weight onto the chair that was behind the desk. He groped his head with both hands and wondered what he was supposed to do next. Fury filled his mind as he considered his next move.

Agent Becker!

Antonio remembered his phone call. He knew that Becker had been found guilty of murder. His connections had worked out well. But now there was another issue. If Antonio was free, he feared that Becker might also have escaped the system and be out on foot by now. He didn't have any time to waste. He needed to find Becker and put him down. After all, it was Becker's fault that he hadn't been with his sick mother when she passed away.

Antonio picked himself up and jetted out the door. Destination: Becker residence.

South Side, Chicago

Operating on autopilot, Freddy led the way, with James a step or two behind. Freddy had it in his head that Antonio had escaped by now and would be making his way home, if not there already. His family was missing, and he had a solid hunch Antonio knew something about it.

James wasn't accustomed to moving through the city streets with a high-powered firearm. The M4 that Freddy gave him was an intimidating rifle. At least it looked that way.

James was clumsy. Not because he had a lack of dexterity, but because he was not used to the tactics of moving from cover to cover to avoid detection. The sounds of gunshots could be heard from all over the city.

Freddy moved from point of cover to point of cover. Each time he was secure behind an area that offered protection, he would look back over his shoulder and wait for James to catch up.

A car horn caused both Freddy and James to jump. The car horn blast was followed by the distinct sound of two vehicles colliding, the metal crunching together at a high rate of speed. They looked and saw an older 1980s truck weaving around the abandoned cars in the street.

The sound of the truck didn't just get their attention, it caught the attention of others, some of whom saw an opportunity as they began to try to get it to stop, each jumping out in front as if the driver would simply stop. One by one, the truck drove over them. It was a grisly thing to observe.

James could tell that Freddy was about to do something stupid, as he'd seen the all too familiar look on his face. "Whatever you're about to do, son, make sure it happens clean."

Freddy heard James's words, and he always took them to heart, but Freddy couldn't get the idea out of his head. *Just one shot,* he thought as he put the butt of the rifle in his shoulder and rested his cheek down. *Just one clean shot and we can take it.*

With his finger on the trigger, he aimed down the sights of the rifle. He carefully placed the front sight tip into the center of the rear sight aperture. He made sure his sight alignment and sight picture were as perfect as he could get, then gently began to apply pressure to the trigger.

The driver was well within shooting distance. *Just a little closer,* he thought. He needed the driver's head to be visible enough to take the shot.

"Are you sure this is what you want to do?" James said, calling doubt into Freddy's mind.

Of course Freddy didn't want to kill the driver, but how else would he be able to save his wife and children? He needed a vehicle. Every minute was precious. Freddy tried to push James's concern to the back of his mind, but he had his own internal demons to wrestle with. What he was about to do would be criminal. The act would mean that clearing his name would be in vain. Freddy began to wonder, *Am I a murderer?* His answer was, of course, no. But then images of his wife and children dominated his judgment and began pushing him into making a hasty decision. Instead of with-drawing the rifle, he held it tightly pulled into his shoulder. The trigger was almost fully to the rear now. As soon as the driver's head could visibly be seen, he could take the shot.

There it is, Freddy thought. The blurry head and face of the driver was now in view. Instead of finishing the trigger pull, he took his focus off the front sight tip of the rifle and put it on the driver. Doing so allowed him to see that the face of the driver was a young woman. Could he do it? Could he pull the trigger and take the life of a woman? He felt a gentle hand on his shoulder. It was James. A reassuring calm flooded Freddy's mind. He released the trigger, grateful that he chose to spare the woman's life.

Freddy lowered the rifle.

He glanced at James and said, "Thank you."

"Sometimes we all need reminding of who we really are," his father-in-law said, giving a calm and reassuring reason amidst the chaos.

A shot rang out.

They looked up just as the truck veered off the street and into a telephone pole.

Two men emerged from down the street, weapons in their hands. Like a young hunter who had just nabbed their first buck, they made haste towards the truck.

"She's still alive," James said.

Cocking his head in the direction of the truck, Freddy confirmed the driver was moving. He glanced back towards the men as they sprinted fast at the truck. On their faces sinister grins told Freddy all he needed to know: these men were evil, and the world would be a better place without them.

"There's that look again," James said.

Operating solely on instinct, Freddy jumped up and went into the street.

"Fritz, what are you doing?"

Freddy raised his rifle, took aim on one of the men, and squeezed the trigger. The 5.56 mm round exploded out of the barrel and passed through the man. He toppled to the ground dead. Freddy pivoted and took aim on the second man, but lost sight of him as he took cover and returned fire.

Freddy advanced, unafraid as bullets zoomed past him. He was laser focused on one thing, killing the man and stopping what he knew would be a lifetime of devilish acts. He spotted the man, aimed, and squeezed off another round. The round just missed, striking the building behind him. It was then that he saw the fear in the man's face, telling Freddy the man had just come to the realization that he'd come face-to-face with a real foe.

Seeing an opportunity, James ran to the passenger side of the truck and pulled up on the handle, to discover it was unlocked. He threw the door open and jumped in. He immediately went to address the woman but was shocked to find she was a teenaged girl, about sixteen if he were to guess. She was no longer moving and to James appeared dead. He checked her pulse and found it was weak. The girl was severely wounded with a visible bullet hole in her head.

James was only versed in advanced first aid, not traumatic brain injuries due to a bullet wound. He stopped what care he was doing and assumed she was on her way out. "God go with you, girl."

Outside, more rounds were exchanged between Freddy and the man until the all too familiar sound of a slide locking to the rear echoed in the street.

A grin stretched across Freddy's face. The man had run out of ammunition. Taking his advantage further, Freddy focused intently on his sights and let a round loose. This time it was true and smashed into the man's head.

Brains, blood, and bits of skull exploded onto the wall behind him. He fell to the ground like a heavy sack, his body making a thud.

Proud that he'd taken out the trash, Freddy confidently strode to the truck and opened the driver's door. Like James, he was shocked to find a teenaged girl. "Is she..."

"Just get in and drive," James barked as he pulled the girl into the center of the bench seat.

Freddy got behind the wheel and handed his rifle to James. "Hold this." He put the truck into reverse and, just before he backed up, muttered, "Please work." He pressed the pedal, and the truck responded with no issue.

The sound of gunfire came from behind them, followed by the ping of the bullets hitting the truck.

"Let's go!" James barked.

Freddy threw the truck into drive and smashed his foot against the accelerator.

The old truck lurched forward, almost stalling.

"C'mon, girl," Freddy said, his tone signaling his fear the truck's engine might have been severely damaged from the crash.

Ting, ting, ting.

"Fritz, let's go!" James howled with fear.

Cautious not to flood the engine, Freddy put pressure on the accelerator enough to get it moving.

The truck edged forward and slowly began to pick up speed.

Confident he could give it more gas, he did.

The truck responded with no issue.

In no time they were speeding down the street.

Freddy looked into the rearview mirror and saw a mob of people in pursuit.

Ting, ting. More bullets struck the truck.

"Watch out!" James yelled, looking up to see a man standing in the middle of the street, a pistol pointed at them.

In unison, they ducked just as the man fired several rounds, each passing through the windshield and out the back window.

Freddy lifted his head just enough to see the man confidently standing in the center of the street. He slammed the accelerator down and pointed the nose of the truck at him.

As if the man were in a trance, he stood his ground, pistol leveled at the truck, firing.

The truck slammed into the man, tossing his body aside like a rag doll.

The girl moaned, "Ahh," as she grabbed the bullet hole in her head.

Freddy and James sat back up in their seats, making eye contact with one another.

"Can you believe it?" Freddy yelled, being the first to respond.

James was unsure what he was supposed to do. "Just focus on the road," he said, encouraging Freddy to drive while he considered his next move.

"Wasn't she shot in the head? I remember seeing a hole in her head!" Freddy yelled.

"She was. I can clearly see a hole," James answered.

"Then what gives?"

"I always said you should believe in miracles."

"We can't care for her. We gotta drop her off somewhere."

"She can't care for herself. Stop acting like those damn savages back there. We're better than them," James reminded his son-in-law.

Frustrated, Freddy grunted, as he knew James was right. "Fine, but she's your responsibility, and if she slows us down too much, I'm dropping her off."

Becker Residence, Chicago

When Antonio arrived, he found the front door open and the screen door hanging by a screw. This was a good sign.

He paused in the doorway, examining the mess and

disorder of the house. He wondered how it came to be and if it had anything to do with what he'd asked for.

Needing to find some sort of confirmation, he stepped across the threshold. "Anyone here?" he called out.

No response.

He walked through the debris, kicking things out of his way. The further he went into the house, the more confident he grew that his wishes had been carried out. He found pleasure in feeling this way. It had been a long time since he'd had some semblance of happiness, and this, this destruction, this chaos, gave him that.

He found himself in the kitchen, and there on the counter was all the proof he needed as well as a piece of critical information that would drive him further to see his revenge fulfilled.

Sitting in plain sight was a handwritten note. He picked it up and read.

Katy, I wish I had time to explain, but I don't. Instead, if you find this letter, please stay here. Me and your dad are out looking for you and will come back. Love, Fritz.

The letter was telling. Freddy had no knowledge of where his wife was. He could sense the panic and fear in the few words; this filled Antonio with such pleasure.

"Now you know how it feels," he sneered. "You destroyed my life, and now I'll destroy yours."

A sudden realization came to his mind. *When was that letter written?* Antonio could gain the upper hand if he played his cards right, but he had to think with clarity.

Freddy said in the letter that he'd return. Maybe a letter of his own was overdue? He rummaged in the drawers until he found a pen, then used it to write a letter where Freddy had left his.

The letter was short and to the point.

Agent Becker, missing someone? I told you that you'd live to regret it. – A.D.

He positioned the note next to the one Freddy had written, then decided not to leave both and picked up the note left for Kaitlyn and shoved it in his pocket for future use.

With his mind set on completing the task of full retribution, he swiftly turned and exited the house. His destination, Rodrigo's house. There he'd not only find the weapons he needed but most likely the one thing Freddy held dear, his wife.

South Side, Chicago

Bodies lined the streets of the neighborhood. It was clear the Latin Kings had made their attack on the area. Rather than leaving the corpses to decay, they'd moved them to the outer perimeter of the 'hood.

"I don't know about this," James said, obviously concerned for their well-being.

The girl grunted and began to squirm.

"I think she's waking," James said, giving the girl a curious glance.

"Well, at the moment, she's just dead weight," Freddy

said, peering over the steering wheel down the street. His mind was quickly assessing the area and formulating a plan.

"This really isn't a good idea."

"James, Katy is probably in this 'hood, and I aim to find her, so please stop this concern."

"You're right."

The click of a pistol's hammer going back sounded to the left of Freddy. He looked and found himself face-to-face with the muzzle of a revolver and an enormously large man holding it.

"Get out of the truck," the man ordered.

Freddy and James both raised their hands.

"Out now!" the man barked.

No choice but to comply, Freddy replied, "I'm going to open the door, and I'll slip out. Just be careful, okay?"

The man had a crazed look upon his face. It was a mixture of fear and excitement.

Slowly, both Freddy and James exited the truck, leaving the girl slumped in the cab.

"I know you," the man snapped as he waved the revolver in Freddy's face.

"Sorry, man, I don't think we're friends," Freddy quipped.

"Yeah, you're, um, you're, ahh, wait, I know, you arrested me a few years back. You're that fucking pig who arrested me," the man said as his tone shifted to anger. He stepped forward and placed the muzzle against Freddy's head.

"Easy, man, I think you're mistaking me for someone else."

"No, it's you. I never forget a face."

"What do you want?" Freddy asked.

The man licked his lips and said, "The truck and all your weapons for a start."

"Keys are in the ignition," Freddy said.

"Let me get the girl out, and then you can –" James said before being interrupted.

"No, leave her," the man said, looking over Freddy's shoulder. "She looks good."

"She's been shot in the head," James snapped back, disgusted by the man's vile comment.

"Even better, the bitch won't fight back," the man said as a devilish sneer stretched across his face.

Freddy's heart was racing. He couldn't just let this man take the truck, but he also couldn't allow him to take the girl, regardless if she was on the verge of dying.

"Just take the truck and our weapons, but please don't harm the girl. Let me get her..." James said, then took a step towards the open passenger door.

With rage in his voice, the man stepped to the side of Freddy and hollered, "Hold it there, old man."

With the man distracted and with clearance, Freddy saw his moment and took it. He reached up, grabbed the man's arm holding the revolver, twisted and pulled it down.

The move worked. The man dropped the pistol, but he was far from defeated. He cocked his left hand and swung. His clenched fist slammed into Freddy's right cheek, sending him staggering to the side a few steps.

Freddy recovered and pounced on the man, who was easily five inches taller and equally wider, with arms like small tree trunks. Freddy knew taking this man in a street brawl wouldn't result in a guaranteed victory, but what other choice did he have?

The two locked arms, then quickly toppled to the ground.

Being the smaller of the two, Freddy swiftly utilized this to his advantage and got on top of the man, but was on his back in no time as the man, who seemed to have incredible strength, merely tossed him off.

James grabbed the rifle from the truck and marched around the truck. "Get off him."

"Shoot the bastard," Freddy cried out as the man's large hands wrapped around Freddy's throat and squeezed.

James raised the rifle, aimed, but couldn't find the courage to pull the trigger. "Get off him or I'll…"

Gasping, Freddy weakly said, "Shoot the mother…"

A gunshot sounded, but it wasn't from James's rifle.

The man let go of Freddy's throat, coughed up blood, and fell to the ground dead.

Coughing and gasping, Freddy looked up and saw the girl with a bullet hole in her head holding his Glock.

"Is he…?" the girl asked.

"Yeah, you killed him, thanks," Freddy said.

She lowered the pistol and stumbled backwards against the truck.

Seeing she wasn't doing well, James stepped towards her.

"No, back off. Get away from me!" she barked and raised the pistol at James. "Drop it."

"But we're..."

"You're what? Huh? I heard you, you wanted to drop me off," she said, now pointing the pistol at Freddy, who was still on the ground.

"I didn't mean –"

She interrupted him and snarled, "This is my daddy's truck, and I'm taking it back."

"We can help you," James said, his rifle now on the ground.

"I have no reason to trust either of you."

"I understand." Freddy sighed as he found himself yet again in a precarious situation. It was like the madness wouldn't end. "Listen, you were shot; I killed the men who did it. We're not here to hurt you. We just need the truck to go find my wife and kids. They've been kidnapped."

"I don't care," she answered, her hands shaking out of fear and weariness.

"We can help each other, okay? How about that?"

"No."

"How about I introduce myself. My name is Freddy. I'm a cop."

"He is," James blurted out.

"What's your name?" Freddy asked.

The girl opened her mouth to reply but hesitated for a moment. "Are you really a cop?"

"Yeah."

"Prove it," she snapped.

"I don't have my badge, but I'm a cop. I'm just trying to find my wife and kids. After we get to where I'm going, you can have the truck, and we'll even help you. Where were you going?"

"I was leaving."

"That's what we plan on doing too, the second I find my wife and kids."

"I'm leaving now."

"But you're alone, a young girl, and you have a hole in your head," Freddy chirped in a mocking tone.

"But I know how to use one of these. I just proved it."

"True, but you'll get further if we work together. Think about it."

She chewed on her lip for a second, then said, "Lori. My name is Lori."

"Nice to meet you, Lori. Now can you please lower the pistol? It's not polite to point weapons at friends."

"We're not friends."

"Then let's just say we're acquaintances who have similar goals," Freddy said.

She thought for a while longer, then slowly lowered the pistol. "Don't try anything."

Freddy jumped to his feet and gave her an amused look. "If we meant to harm you, we would've done it by now."

That made sense to her.

"Now can we get back to the task at hand...finding my family?"

De LaRosa Residence, South Side, Chicago

"I don't care. I'm going to take a look," James growled, using a strict parental tone as he stood, hands on hips, in front of Lori.

"I'm fine," she snapped back.

"You don't look fine, and you have a hole in your head."

Lori stiff-armed him, then walked away to go find food.

"Whoever was here seems to have cleared out already," Freddy said as he quickly cleared the rooms. "There's nothing, and no sign Katy or the kids were ever here."

Seeing the concerned look on Freddy's face, James approached and put a comforting hand on his shoulder. "We'll find them. I just know we will."

A loud crash sounded in the kitchen.

"Lori?" Freddy called out.

He and James ran into the kitchen to find Lori on the floor, her body flopping.

"What do I do?" James asked.

"Just keep her from bumping her head. It looks like she's having a seizure."

James positioned himself at her head and Freddy at her feet.

"God, she's got a fever," James said.

"We gotta find a way to get her core temp down."

"Without water, that's going to be tough."

"I'll check the freezer. Maybe there's still something cold

in there," Freddy said, jumping to his feet. He threw open the freezer, to find it empty. "Shit."

"Let's get her outside," James suggested.

With care and ease, they lifted and carried her outside. As luck would have it, a cold breeze was whipping through the neighborhood.

After a few agonizing minutes, Lori's seizure subsided. She opened her eyes and asked, "What happened?"

"You were doing the funky chicken," James joked.

Lori looked at him, confused by what he said.

"You had a seizure, and you have a fever," Freddy explained.

"We need to find a pharmacy or something. She needs something for the fever," James said.

Freddy motioned with his head for the two to step aside and talk out of earshot of Lori. Taking the cue, James got up and walked over to a tree about ten feet from Lori, who was lying still on the ground.

"She's slowing us down," Freddy said.

"I'm not going to just leave her," James fired back.

"James, we're looking for your daughter and grandkids. Why are you giving this stranger such priority?"

"I'm not, this is just the decent thing to do, and I pray, I do, that someone is showing Katy and the kids the same level of graciousness and humanity."

Freddy was growing frustrated by the entire situation. "She was shot in the head. She's just a dead girl walking. It's time to just leave her comfortable and move on."

"No."

"Then stay, you stay here. Care for her, and I'll return for you two later," Freddy offered.

"No."

"Damn it, Dad, we're wasting time."

"I'm fine. Let's get going," Lori yelped.

The two men looked back and saw she was sitting up, rubbing her head.

"You know, what if she wasn't shot? I mean, where's the exit wound?" James asked.

"But she has a hole in her head. It's clear as day," Freddy snapped back.

Ignoring Freddy, James walked over to Lori and knelt. "Can I please take a look at your head?"

Too weary to argue, Lori lowered her head.

Cradling her head gently in his hands, he looked at it carefully. "Get me that bottle of water in the truck."

"There's a first aid kit in there too," Lori said.

"Then get that," James ordered Freddy.

Agitated, Freddy dug in the truck until he found the small red first aid kit. He returned to James and handed it to him.

James opened it and rummaged through until he found the antiseptic wipes. He tore one open and cleaned the dried blood from around the wound.

Freddy immediately became paranoid because of the environment. It was a bad neighborhood, and with everything else going on, he needed to watch his back.

"What now?" James asked.

"Let's get her in the truck and get out of here," Freddy answered. He was confident he wasn't going to find anything that would give him a clue about his family there, and the best thing for him now was to move on to the next location.

"You sure?"

"Yeah, let's get the hell out of this shithole."

Gently they moved Lori back into the truck. Paranoid that he was being watched, Freddy looked one last time out across the plain of buildings. Nothing. He started the truck, and the three of them left South Deering for Freddy's home.

"A pharmacy. Maybe we can stop and get Lori some ibuprofen. We need something to get her fever down."

"I suppose it can't hurt to stop and get other things too," Freddy said, turning the wheel in the direction of the pharmacy.

South Side, Chicago

Ricco had fallen asleep watching over Kaitlyn, who, on the other hand, hadn't slept since she'd been taken.

Each time she had felt the pull of fatigue, she either forced herself to stay awake or her nightmares prevented her. Her life felt forfeit, as each hour, minute or second was nothing but torture. Her eyes watched as Ricco's chest rose and fell with each breath he took. She knew he wasn't a good man, but he wasn't evil like the others. Anxiety was building in her, as she knew Ricco's watch would end soon, and with it came more terror.

Bam, the door flew open.

Ricco jolted awake and stood, surprised that he had dozed off. He worried that he'd been caught. The man at the door was Mendez, Estevan's number one. He was looking straight at Kaitlyn. Ricco feared for her but was relieved that he hadn't seen him sleeping. That would be bad. Very bad.

"Get her cleaned up and brought to the front room. Somebody's here to see her." He then turned and walked out.

Ricco looked concerned, and Kaitlyn could see it in his eyes.

She mumbled.

"Don't start. If somebody is here to see you, you'd best be on good behavior."

Kaitlyn feared the worst. She began pulling at her restraints, as if she had a chance of escape if she could break free.

"Just stop," Ricco said. "These people will kill you. Then who's gonna care for those bambinos of yours, huh?"

Ricco untied her legs, expecting her to kick and put up a fight, but she didn't. He went for her hands, then paused to give her one final word of warning. "If you try anything stupid, they will kill you and possibly your little ones. Do you understand?"

Kaitlyn nodded.

He untied her hands and stood back.

She was too sore to move, and her arms and legs were cramping from being tied. She attempted to stand but couldn't. A combination of fatigue and pain spread across her weary body.

"Take my hand," Ricco said, offering his right hand.

She gave him a sad look, lifted her hand, and placed it in his.

He took hold of it and with his other hand grabbed her arm. He lifted her gently to her feet. Standing face-to-face, he saw the damage of the rape and torture on her swollen and bruised face. He pulled a handkerchief from his back pocket, doused it with water, and carefully wiped the dried blood from her nose and lips.

Grateful for his tenderness, she stood on wobbly legs. She had thoughts of fleeing, but she knew there was no escape. She had nowhere to go, and if she could make a break for it, she'd be leaving her children.

She was stuck and had to pray that the others would begin to show her mercy like Ricco had.

"Come on, now. Play it cool," he told her one last time.

She nodded.

He led her out of the room and around the corner to the right. From there, they turned left and walked through the kitchen. Hordes of food caches were in stacks all over the countertops. The cabinets were full, and stacks of canned goods covered the floor against the walls.

To the left of the kitchen, several men were standing in the living room, their eyes glued on her. One of them stood out. He had tattoos of teardrops under his eyes. Another tattoo of two letters, *LK*, was on one side of his throat, and on the other side was a crown.

"This is her, Carbolla," Estevan said.

"Why's she all busted up?" he asked. His tone signaled to Kaitlyn that he had some power and influence.

"They've been raping and beating me," she cried out, unable to maintain control of her emotions.

Rodrigo turned to Estevan. "Is this true?"

All the men began looking at one another. Rodrigo realized that each of them knew something and they weren't talking.

Rodrigo was never a law-abiding citizen. From his youth he was in and out of the judicial system. By the time he was fifteen, he was being charged as an adult for murder. But even he had rules, and obeying them was critical in his eyes. He turned back to Estevan. "I gave you very specific orders, did I not?"

"*Jefe*, the power went out, and I didn't think you were gonna make it home."

Rodrigo looked at him in silence, waiting for him to add something else to the story, but nothing came. "So you think because the power is out, we don't have to follow rules, Estevan?" Rodrigo extended his hand to Carlos, who was standing closest, his palm facing up. His gaze was fixed on Estevan with intent and focus.

Carlos pulled a pistol from his waistband and placed it into Rodrigo's hand.

Kaitlyn whimpered under her breath, as she feared something horrible was about to happen and she'd be forced to witness it.

"Answer my question, Estevan," Rodrigo barked, gripping the pistol tightly as he stood.

The two were locked in a frightful stare.

"I'm sorry," Estevan answered, his voice cracking.

Without hesitation, Rodrigo placed the pistol under Estevan's jaw.

"I'm sorry, it won't –"

Rodrigo pulled the trigger.

The pistol fired, causing the top of Estevan's head to explode. Brains and blood splattered the ceiling, with some spraying the others, including Kaitlyn, who was standing just feet away.

Estevan's body dropped heavily to the floor, smashing a glass coffee table on the way down.

Kaitlyn began screaming uncontrollably, followed by the muffled screams of the children in the back room.

"I gave one order to Estevan," Rodrigo said. "That was to kidnap Agent Becker's wife and hide her at my place. That was it. No rape. No abuse. Nothing about kids. So what is it that I'm hearing in the back?"

"Her kids, Carbolla," Ricco answered. "Becker's son and daughter."

Rodrigo began pacing the room, his mind spinning with what he should do about the kids. He hated hurting children, both physically and psychologically. He considered those who did weak. He stopped in front of Ricco, craned his head, and stared into his dark brown eyes. "Please tell me you had nothing to do with taking those children. Please tell me nothing has happened to them. I swear to God, if I see one mark on them –"

"Nothing's happened to them to the best of my knowledge. I had no part in taking them. I was making loot runs when they were picked up by Carlos and Mendez."

Rodrigo looked to Mendez.

"Estevan told us to take the woman and kids, right, Carlos?" Mendez said frantically, looking to Carlos for confirmation.

"That's right," Carlos replied, his tone riddled with fear.

Kaitlyn was on the floor by this point, her sobs echoing loudly in the small space. She had gotten so worked up she had become hysterical.

Distracted, Rodrigo glanced at her and snapped, "Somebody get her out of here and bring me the kids."

Ricco picked her up off the floor and escorted her to the back room.

Along the way through the kitchen, she reached out with her hand, when Ricco wasn't watching close enough, and knocked over a stack of canned goods.

The cans crashed to the floor.

"I'm sorry," she said, crying beneath her words. She bent over to pick the items up.

"No, I'll get it," he said, bending over to pick them up.

Seeing an opportunity, Kaitlyn reached for a knife on the

counter and quickly grabbed it. She tucked it in her waistband and stood quietly.

Ricco picked up the last can and set it on the counter. Frustrated, he sighed. "Let's go." Then he took her back to the room.

Carbolla's Residence, South Side, Chicago

Antonio walked up toward the porch of Rodrigo's home just in time to see Mendez and Carlos dumping Estevan's body on the front porch. He recognized the two from common acquaintances but couldn't say he knew them. He was excited, as he knew they knew Rodrigo. "Hey, I'm here to see –"

Before he could finish his sentence, Mendez pulled his pistol from his waistband and pointed it at him. "Who the hell are you?"

"Put that down," Antonio replied, his hands in the air. "I ain't putting nothin' down. Who are you?"

"I'm here to see Rodrigo."

"I don't give a shit."

"I'm Antonio. I just got out of prison."

Mendez cocked his head, then shot Carlos a look. "What do you think?"

"Lower it, homie. I recognize him," Carlos said, stepping towards Antonio. "Yo, how did you get out?"

"The same as everyone else. I just walked out as soon as the power went out."

"What do you want with Rodrigo?"

"I'm here about Becker."

Mendez and Carlos again looked at each other.

"You know what I'm talking about, don't you?" Antonio asked.

"You'd better come with us," Carlos said.

MICHAEL AND KAYLEIGH stood before Rodrigo, their arms bound and mouths gagged. The two children shook with fear and whimpered pleas for help and mercy.

Upon seeing them, Rodrigo was sickened. "Untie them, now!"

Ricco jumped to the task, removed the bindings and ungagged them.

"Is this the man who took you from your home?" Rodrigo asked, pointing to Ricco.

Ricco's heart rate escalated rapidly. He didn't know these kids and they didn't know him. He quickly said a prayer, hoping they wouldn't mistakenly name him as one of their captors.

Michael and Kayleigh both shook their heads.

"It appears it's your lucky day," Rodrigo sneered at Ricco.

The sound of the front door slamming was followed by Mendez and Carlos entering the front room with Antonio in tow.

"Carbolla," Mendez said, "this man says he blooded in?"

Rodrigo didn't have a chance to answer before the kids pointed at Mendez and Carlos. "He took us," they said.

"Carbolla, we already told you we were told to take them."

Rodrigo turned back to the kids. "Did they hurt you in any way?"

"No," they answered in unison.

"It's also your lucky day," Rodrigo said to Mendez and Carlos. He stood up, brushed past them, and walked up to Antonio. "What's up, De LaRosa? I didn't think you had what it takes to get out."

"I'm here, aren't I," he answered, short and to the point. "I think Becker may be on his way here soon."

Rodrigo turned back to Ricco and pointed at the kids. "Get them out of here. They don't need to hear this."

"Dad's gonna come and save us," Michael snapped.

Kayleigh was bolstered by her brother's courage. "You should just turn yourselves in now," she added.

"I like these kids," Rodrigo said with a shit-eating grin. Ricco whisked the kids away before they could say anything else.

Rodrigo turned back to Antonio. "Tell me what you know."

"I went to Becker's house to make sure you fulfilled your end of the deal."

"You doubt my integrity?"

"Not at all, but the power went out, and there's talk of a new world order and people holding signs out on the street that read '*the end is here.*'"

"So you thought all that would change my mind? I took care of this before the lights went out. I told you I would take care of you, and I have. Now you gotta take care of the pack."

"Take care of the pack?"

"You belong to the Kings now. If you don't do what you're told, you'll end up like Estevan. Do I make myself clear?"

"And what happened to Estevan?" Antonio asked, curious if the body Mendez and Carlos had been carrying was him.

"He's dead because he didn't know how to follow orders," Rodrigo clarified. He cleared his throat and continued, "What did you find at Becker's house that leads you to believe he's coming here?"

"He left a letter on the counter for his wife."

"She's here and safely tucked away in the back room."

"Safely?"

"Her kids are here, too. I don't remember promising you anything involving children. I don't deal with kids."

"She's gotta die, Carbolla," Antonio insisted.

"Did you hear what I just said? Her kids are here, too. Estevan brought them all here. I ain't about to leave those kids as orphans."

"Becker left me orphaned. I asked for something poetic."

Rodrigo stepped away and began to pace the room. He stopped and looked at Mendez and Carlos. "I want the two of you to stand guard outside. Gather your brothers if you think you need it."

Mendez and Carlos did as they were asked.

With the room empty save for them, Rodrigo asked. "Now, tell me, why would you think he's coming here?"

"I know Becker, and I know he won't stop until he finds her. It's best we end her now and dump her body on his lawn."

"And the kids? He'll keep looking for them, too."

"We can't let them go – they know too much. If they survive the trip home, they'll lead Becker right back here."

"Then we keep them here – until the storm blows over, but for the record, I think you're wrong about killing the woman. Becker arresting you and your mom dying aren't connected. That's not on him, that's just...what do you say, dumb luck."

"Respectfully, I disagree," he said and walked past Rodrigo to the back room, where he hoped to find Becker's wife. He turned the knob and pushed the door open, to find she was gone, and Ricco was dead. "Carbolla!" Antonio shouted.

Hearing the urgency in his call, Rodrigo ran to the room. His face contorted with anger.

Antonio rushed to the next room, where the kids had been kept, only to find duct tape and rope lying on the floor, but no kids. He bent down and picked up the duct tape to find blood. "She killed Ricco and used the knife to cut her kids free. She couldn't have gotten far," Rodrigo said. He stood up and turned to Antonio. "We can catch her, and when we do, she dies."

South Side, Chicago

Kaitlyn, Michael, and Kayleigh ran for their lives.

Not familiar with the streets around her, she headed east, hoping to run into or at least see Lake Michigan. From there, she knew all she had to do was head north.

She knew they would find Ricco and soon come looking for her. This was a do-or-die moment. She and the kids either made it to safety or died trying, but where was safety? She couldn't go home, no, they would expect that, and that was where they'd found her to begin with. She needed a place, but where? Her mind was moving slowly although her heart raced. She fought against the confusion and panic that lay on the edges of her nerves. She couldn't surrender to her emotions now, no, she needed to think clearly, but as she tried, she found herself flustered.

The kids didn't utter a word. They ran alongside her, their heavy breaths telling Kaitlyn they too knew the urgency of the moment.

She continuously looked over her shoulder to see if they were being chased, but each time saw no one.

Knowing she couldn't go home, another place popped into her head. Her father's house. Yes, she'd go there. Her captors didn't know his house, and hopefully he was there. To her left she recognized some mid-rise buildings in the distance, then saw just beyond that the high-rises. She had a good idea of where she was. "This way!" she said to the kids just as she turned left down a long street. Around abandoned vehicles they ran, her head swiveling back to ensure they weren't being followed.

Kayleigh let out a scream and stopped.

Jumping from the surprise, Kaitlyn stopped too and saw the bodies lining the streets along the sidewalk. "Kayleigh, come, we don't have time to waste."

Kayleigh was frozen in fear.

"Honey, please, let's go," Kaitlyn pleaded.

"Mommy, I'm scared."

"It's going to be alright."

"Where are we going?" Michael asked.

"Grandpa's house," she answered. "Now, Kayleigh, we have to keep moving, c'mon."

Kayleigh took a few steps, reached out with her hand and whimpered.

Kaitlyn reached too, took a hold of Kayleigh's hand, and pulled her close. The two embraced.

"I'm so scared, Mommy."

Caressing her, Kaitlyn softly said, "We're going to be okay, but we do need to keep moving. We can't stop. Okay?"

"But I'm scared."

"I know you are, but right now I need you to be strong. Can you do that for me?"

Kayleigh whimpered.

"Can you?"

Kayleigh nodded.

"That's my good girl."

"I think we should go," Michael said, looking around at the few people who were staring at them.

"Good idea," Kaitlyn replied.

A few onlookers began to close the distance as others started to catcall and make obscene gestures.

The three took off at a healthy sprint, turned a corner, and ran directly into a wall of men. By their attire they were gang members.

"Where are you going in a hurry?" one man said as he stepped towards them.

Kaitlyn and the kids turned around to flee the way they came, but the men had encircled them.

She faced the first man and said, "Please, we're just trying to get home."

The man approached. He was now inches from her face. He reached up and touched her hair. "Home? How about you come home with me?"

"No, no, man, she's coming with me," another man said, pushing the first to the side.

Kaitlyn knew things could only escalate from here. Both Michael and Kayleigh clung tightly to their mother's arms.

"Sweet thing, where are you coming from in such a rush?" another one asked.

She searched her mind for a quick and snappy answer. She came up empty so went with the cliché response. "My husband will be here soon."

The men laughed. "Husband? If he cared about you, don't you think he'd be here now?"

"Please," she begged. "We're just passing through."

"This is Bloods territory now. If you wanna pass, you'll have to pay the toll."

Kaitlyn knew exactly where this was going. She knew the cost would be more than she could pay with money. She weighed the price of passage against her own dignity. In the end, motherhood would win the day.

Kaitlyn stooped down and gathered her kids in close. "You guys remember how to get to Papa James's house from here?"

Michael looked around to survey the area. He felt confident that he could take up the mantle of leadership. "I remember."

She kissed them both on the cheek and whispered in their ears.

The Bloods watched as the woman sent her children away and she stayed behind. The bargain had been made, and the offer had been accepted. They let the kids pass.

Chicago

Lori opened her eyes to see the light of day had rapidly faded. Her head pounded with pain. It didn't help that Freddy was driving like a madman.

"Where are we?" she asked, sitting up and squinting out the window.

"We're still in Chicago," James answered.

Lori grabbed her head. "How am I even alive?"

"That's a good question," Freddy answered, turning his focus from his search for just a moment. "The bullet's still in there. It's why you have a fever."

"Here, swallow these," James said, handing her a bottle of Tylenol.

"Is this supposed to help my pain?"

"It's acetaminophen. It's a fever reducer."

Lori happily accepted the gift. She looked back over her shoulder into the bed of the truck, halfway expecting to see Freddy's family. They weren't there. "No luck?"

"Nothing yet. I thought I'd check out everything between the jail and my home. You know – just in case my wife came looking for me."

"We're on our way to his house now," James answered.

Lori noticed she was wearing James's flannel shirt. "Thanks," she said, with a half smile.

"You're welcome."

"So how much farther to your house?" she asked Freddy.

"That's it right there," he said, pulling into the driveway.

"You gotta nice home," she said as Freddy put the truck in park.

Freddy scanned the house for a brief moment and sensed something was off. He grabbed his rifle and jumped out of the truck, leaving the door open.

"What is it?"

"Something isn't right."

"Wait for me," James said. He got out of the truck as fast as he could and raced to catch up to Freddy.

"I'll just wait here, then," Lori quipped. She watched the two disappear into the house, then rested her head back. She adjusted to get comfortable in the seat, turned her head, and caught sight of the keys dangling from the ignition.

FREDDY TOOK point as James followed behind. The house was empty, but Freddy's note to Kaitlyn was gone. His heart leaped inside. For a split second he thought that his wife had been home and found his note. He was wrong. Freddy picked up the note and looked at it. It wasn't his wife's writing. It was something worse. Much worse.

"What is it?" James asked, seeing the expression change on Freddy's face.

"It's from Tony De LaRosa."

"The man you suspected of taking Katy and the kids?"

"Yep."

James was shocked to find that Freddy had been right all along. His investigative senses were prime. "We were just in his house. He wasn't there. Katy and the kids weren't there."

"He had them taken. It's the only thing that makes sense at this point. He was locked up. He couldn't have coordinated this after the EMP. He had to have made it happen while he was locked up. That means that one of his thug friends may very well have them."

"But there's no way to know for sure."

"We've already been over this, Pops. There's no way to

know anything anymore, but what else am I supposed to go on?"

"I think we should head back to my place. Just in case. Maybe Katy and the kids went there for safety. Maybe all this hunting is in vain."

"What's the point in heading back to your place? He was here. Antonio De LaRosa was here – in my home! I can find him. I'll find them."

"I can't help but hear you always on this rant about finding this De LaRosa character and clearing your name. It just seems that your priorities are a bit skewed."

"My top priority is to find my family, but if I can clear my name while doing so, then so be it."

"I just don't want –"

Before James could finish, Freddy cut him off. "We don't have time for this. Every second wasted is another second something could happen to them." Freddy marched towards the front door.

Following closely behind, James asked, "What's the plan? Where are we going?"

Freddy dropped his head and shook it with frustration. "We're not going anywhere, at least not in the truck."

James emerged from the house and looked over Freddy's shoulder to see the truck was gone and so was Lori. "Maybe I should have stayed in the truck."

"Too late now," Freddy said. He cleared the front steps and began to head down the street.

"Where are you going?"

"Your house."

———

FREDDY AND JAMES were feet away from their destination when a bloodcurdling scream stopped them in their tracks. At first Freddy hesitated, but his conscience had the best of him.

"It came from over there," Freddy said, pointing to a house down the street.

"Is that the truck?" James asked, his neck craned forward as he squinted to get a better look.

Freddy recognized it too and took off for it with James in tow. A slight but recognizable limp distinguished his gait.

The truck was empty and the keys weren't in the ignition.

Once again, Freddy found himself in a dilemma. The call to duty was strong. So strong that it tended to overcome him at every calling.

Another scream bellowed out, this time closer.

"The house," Freddy said and ran towards it, his rifle at the ready.

"Wait up," James complained.

Unconcerned for his own safety, Freddy pulled the storm door open and entered the house, to find a man in a green winter coat on top of Lori.

Lori struggled as best she could, but the man was too strong for her.

Hearing the door open, the man stood to confront Freddy.

Seizing the opportunity, Lori stood up and ran behind Freddy, using him as a shield.

Unarmed, the man suddenly realized he was outmatched, outnumbered, and outgunned.

"I don't want any trouble. I was just trying to have a little fun before I die."

Freddy pointed his rifle at the man. "I can take care of that, right here, right now!"

The man threw his hands into the air. "Please, mister, don't kill me."

"Kill him," Lori shouted. "Shoot his face off."

Freddy's training taught him to take the high road and to avoid violence where possible. He had obviously broken the law. Battery. Assault. Freddy had seen this kind of thing before. Since the rape hadn't technically occurred, the man would most likely get off without so much as a slap on the wrist.

"Grab something to tie him up with," Freddy ordered, not caring who did it.

"Tie him up?" Lori shouted in disbelief. "He tried to rape me. He's gotta die."

"No one is dying right now," Freddy snapped back.

"He will do it again. I thought you said you were a cop," Lori barked.

"I am, and cops don't murder people."

The man chuckled. "Some do."

Freddy gave him a hard stare and exclaimed, "I'm willing to change my mind."

James looked around and saw an extension cord. He pulled it from the wall and approached the man. "Don't try anything stupid."

"I won't."

James tied the man's arms behind his back and shoved him to the floor. "Now just sit there and count your blessings."

"I can't believe you're not going to take him out. The man is vile; he's evil. How many other women has he raped? He'll just do it again the second he gets free," Lori blasted Freddy.

"I don't have time for this," Freddy snapped back. "Now where are the keys to the truck?"

She lifted her arm and pointed at the man. "He has them."

"Where are they?"

The man nodded with his head. "My coat pocket."

James was still next to him, so he bent down and reached into his pocket. He flinched and pulled his hand out. "Ouch."

"Be careful, there's..."

James reached in again and removed a dirty needle.

"Sorry," the man said with a sneer.

Angered and having reached his threshold, Freddy stepped up to the man and struck him with the butt of his rifle.

The man fell onto his back, unconscious, a bloody gash now on his forehead from where the butt of the rifle had struck him.

James dug into the pocket again, and this time found the

keys. He tossed them to Freddy and stood up. He examined the pinprick on his finger and grunted. "I hope he doesn't have any diseases."

"I'm sure he does," Lori crowed with disgust.

"C'mon, let's get out of here," Freddy said. He turned and exited the house.

A gunshot rang out a few seconds later.

Freddy ran back into the house just as Lori was coming out, the rifle in her hands. She gave it to Freddy and said, "Since you couldn't do what was right, I did."

"She grabbed the rifle before I could –" James protested before Freddy interrupted him.

On the floor the man lay, a pool of blood around his head.

Freddy looked back over his shoulder and watched as Lori got into the truck and closed the door. He had to admit that he wasn't sad that a vile man was dead, but at the same time he wasn't happy about it either. He still believed in the rule of law, and she had just murdered a man without a fair trial. He rushed from the house, stopping just outside the truck window. "You shouldn't have done that."

"I don't know you, but I know that he was a bad man, and if we're going to survive in this new world, we're going to have to adapt."

"Who the hell are you?" Freddy asked rhetorically.

"Are we going or not?" she asked, her arms folded across her chest in a defiant posture.

James arrived at the truck. "What do we do with her?"

"Nothing," Freddy replied. He got in the truck and

slammed the door shut. He looked at Lori and asked, "Are you going to behave going forward?"

"If you mean will I take my truck and run off again? Then no, I'm here to stay if you let me."

James got into the truck and gave Lori a skeptical look. "She makes me nervous now."

"She's the least of my worries. Let's get going," Freddy said, starting the truck and speeding off.

The drive to James's house was short, just a single city block and they were there.

"Everything seems to be in place," James said, looking over his property.

The three of them exited the truck.

"I gave Katy a key to my house years ago. If she has it on her, she might be inside," James said, walking up with his own keys in his hand.

Freddy too looked over the house and saw no signs of forced entry.

James unlocked the door and threw it open. "Katy, kids, are you here?" he called out.

No answer.

"Katy?" he called out. He went from the front room to the kitchen but found nothing and no one.

Freddy rushed in. "Michael? Kayleigh?"

Silence.

James turned to Lori. "Go check the toolshed. It's around back and it's unlocked."

Lori, who was standing in the doorway at this point, took

off toward the backyard.

"Hello?" she said softly, listening for a reply, but like inside, there was no response. She threw open the latch on the weathered toolshed door and opened it. She jumped back when she saw two small kids holding each other inside. She regained her composure and asked, "Are you Michael and Kayleigh?"

The kids nodded.

"I found them. They're here!" Lori cried out. She advanced, but the kids recoiled further inside and took shelter behind the mower.

"Leave us alone!" Michael said as he held up a large crescent wrench.

"I'm not here to harm you. I'm a friend of your dad's."

"I don't believe you," Michael spat. His trust of adults was at an all-time low.

Having heard Lori, Freddy burst from the back door, leapt off the steps, and sprinted to the toolshed. He pushed past Lori to see Michael and Kayleigh. "You're alive."

The kids stood up and ran into his open arms.

Tears flowed as the three embraced.

Freddy kissed them repeatedly.

James appeared in the doorway. "Oh, thank goodness."

Pulling back to get a good look at them, he asked, "Are you hurt?"

In unison the two replied, "No."

"Where's your mom?" he asked.

"She's paying a toll," Kayleigh answered.

"Paying a toll?"

Fearing the worst, "Can you show me?" Freddy asked.

They nodded and took him tightly by the hand, leading him outside.

IT TOOK Freddy only a moment to understand what had happened to his wife and where she was.

With Lori and James bundled in the back of the truck and the kids up front in the cab, Freddy headed for the area where Kaitlyn was last seen.

In the bed of the truck, James held his rifle tightly, his fingers in a white-knuckled grip. Freddy had given him enough information to know they were probably headed into a firefight. To say he was scared was an understatement.

"There she is. That's Mom," Michael exclaimed.

His fears washed away the second he laid eyes on her. Needing to get to her as fast as he could, he smashed his foot down on the accelerator. He pulled up alongside and cried out, "Kaitlyn!"

He threw the truck into park and jumped out, the kids right behind him. The two embraced tightly.

"I thought I lost you," he whispered into her ear as he tightened his hold on her.

Kaitlyn sobbed, and her knees grew weak.

Freddy could smell smoke and cannabis – scents that he was all too familiar with, scents that shouldn't be coming from his wife. The smells confused him at first. He pulled away to give her a quick look-over. Her pants were wet, an obvious telltale sign of what she had endured. Then he understood *the toll*. He pulled her in again, unsure if he could hold her tighter. Remorse, disgust, sorrow, failure, anger, hate, loss, pain – these were just a small sample of the emotions that washed over him.

James stood silently in the background, taking in everything, a grin on his face, knowing that they had been successful in their quest. He knew something had gone terribly wrong, but now wasn't the time or place to ask questions.

Lori exited the bed of the truck and walked up beside James. "I'm guessing that's the wifey?" she asked, in a light-hearted tone.

"That's her. That's my daughter, Katy."

Pettigrew Residence, Chicago

Ryan and Janie had no family in Chicago or in the surrounding rural areas. With no place to go, Ryan had decided to stay and fortify his house for what appeared to be a long haul.

Janie was uneasy about surrendering her fate to the safety of a few two-by-fours and brick walls. She didn't have the police training Ryan had, but even with that, she felt uneasy and decided she would try to convince him.

"We can't survive like this for long. We only have enough

food to last us a couple of weeks. After that, we'll have to leave in search of food. We don't even know if the water's running," she said, walking to the kitchen sink. She turned the faucet on and watched it run empty. It wasn't until that moment that she wished she would have captured the water.

Ryan was too busy nailing boards to the walls to engage Janie in an argument over the future.

She wasn't done making her argument though. "I think we should leave and find Katy and the kids. She's out there alone."

Ryan got a crazy look in his eyes. So much so that he stopped what he was doing and gazed at her. "We got this. We don't need anybody's help."

"I'm just saying we need to pool our resources. We can survive longer like that."

Ryan went back to hammering. "The answer's *no*," he insisted.

Frustrated at his behavior, Janie gave up on her dispute, but she wasn't going to let it rest in the long run. She was confused at Ryan's lack of interest in joining forces with the Beckers. After all, Ryan and Fritz had been friends for many years. There was something off about how he was acting, but she chalked it up to the stress of the events unfolding.

"Why are you so against it?" she asked.

"Because there's three more mouths to feed if we take them in. We only have enough for us."

"I get that, but what if they need our help? What if they're in trouble? And they might have food or other supplies.

Having extra hands and stuff might outweigh the extra mouths. Plus with Fritz locked up, I'm sure they'd welcome the company and security."

"He's locked up for murder, Janie," he said, turning to glare at her again.

"You don't believe he did it, do you?"

"It doesn't matter what I believe. He was convicted in a court of law. That's the end of the story."

Frustrated, Janie stormed off, leaving Ryan to finish boarding up the windows.

"LET'S GO, PEOPLE," Freddy barked.

Back and forth everyone went from James's house to the truck, with arms full of supplies.

"Stack everything back near the tailgate," Freddy said, putting in a box full of canned goods. In his peripheral vision he saw movement and looked up to see a familiar face – Antonio De LaRosa – crossing the street just a few houses down.

Freddy went to the cab and grabbed his rifle. He took a few steps then stopped. What was the plan? Go down and shoot him? Why? He'd gotten his family back; wasn't that all he wanted?

Watching Freddy, James came up. "You know him?"

"Yeah, that's De LaRosa."

"And what do you plan on doing?"

"I should go kill him," Freddy said. "But I won't."

Overhearing their conversation, Kaitlyn exclaimed, "You should go end this."

Shocked to know Kaitlyn had heard, Freddy faced her. "It has ended. I have you and the kids now. All I'd be doing is taking a big risk. No, I won't go."

"He had people take me and the kids. They raped me!" Kaitlyn fired back, anger rising in her.

"He's right, Katy, there's nothing to be done. That man will find the Lord will serve retribution."

"If you're not willing to do it, then I will," Kaitlyn said as she reached for the rifle.

"No," Freddy said, holding the rifle just out of her reach.

"They raped me, Fritz."

"I know they hurt you, but me murdering him only puts me...us at risk. I don't know if I'd be walking into an ambush."

"Coward."

Freddy recoiled from her comment.

"Nice truck," a voice sounded from the side of the house.

The three looked over and saw a man step out with a pistol to Lori's head.

Freddy raised his rifle but froze when he heard slides racking and hammers cocking back all around them. He looked and now saw more men. They were gang members, and he now wondered if Antonio was behind it.

"Drop it and get on your knees," the first man said.

"Don't do it," Lori growled.

The man pressed the muzzle firmly against Lori's temple and snapped back, "You shut it."

Enraged, Lori slammed her heel against the top of the man's foot.

The man howled in pain.

Lori went for the pistol, and with that, a fight broke out.

Seeing an opportunity, Freddy pulled his Glock from his waistband, but before he could bring it up and take aim, he was hit on the back of the head. The blow dropped him to his knees. He attempted to recover, but another strike took him. He slammed face-first onto the hard ground and passed out.

FREDDY WOKE to find James hovering over him.

"Oh, good, I feared you were dead," James said, his face battered and bleeding.

Freddy sat up and looked around. He saw the truck was gone, and the kids were on the steps of the house, crying. He kept scanning but didn't see Kaitlyn. "Where is she?"

"They took her," James replied.

"What?" Freddy asked and got to his feet. "Where...where did they take her?"

"I don't know, I just woke up myself," James answered, his face showing not only the beating but his deep sorrow.

"We need to find her," Freddy exclaimed as he looked around for a weapon.

"They traded her, at least that's what the kids said."

"Traded...what does that mean?" Freddy asked. He marched over to the kids, who sat sobbing. "What do you mean she was traded?"

"Maybe they took her back," Kayleigh said in between heavy sobs.

"Take her back...where, take her back where?" Freddy asked, his tone frantic.

"Back where they had us before," Kayleigh replied.

"And where is that? Can you take me there?"

Michael gave his best explanation of where they had been taken before. It was enough for Freddy to know where he was going. Freddy turned his head back to James. "What about Lori?"

James shook his head. "She didn't make it," he said with a sorrowful voice.

Freddy looked around and saw Lori's body lying off to the side of the house.

"She put up a hell of a fight," James said. "Just before I was knocked out, I saw them put a bullet in her head."

"We can't let this stand," Freddy said in anger.

"We have no choice, son. The evil deeds of those men will come back on them. It's not for us to determine their fate. God will deal with them on His own timetable."

Freddy dismissed the sermon and headed towards his house.

"Where are you going?"

"To get more guns," Freddy answered.

STANDING in front of his gun cabinet for the second time that day, Freddy pulled out a Glock 19 and his last AR-platform rifle. He turned and handed the M4 to James along with a box of .223 ammunition and two spare thirty-round magazines.

He grabbed two extra magazines for the Glock and shoved them into his pocket. "That's it," he said before spotting another piece of equipment, a range finder. He grabbed it and shoved it into a backpack. "We're going to need this, too," he said, placing it into the backpack.

James stood, but his mind was preoccupied.

"What is it?" Freddy asked.

"Did you hear that?" James asked.

"No."

"Someone is upstairs."

Freddy rounded up Michael and Kayleigh and hid them in the rear of the basement beneath the stairwell. "I need you two to stay here and hide. Don't come out, and don't make any sounds. You have to remain absolutely silent. Do you understand?"

Michael and Kayleigh nodded their heads in agreement.

With the kids tucked away, Freddy returned to James, who was listening intently to the walking sounds coming from up above.

"I'm going up first. Stay just behind me, okay?"

James nodded.

Taking the lead, Freddy pointed his pistol up the stairwell and began his ascent slowly.

The door above him opened.

Freddy aimed the pistol and began to squeeze.

"Freddy?"

Taking a second look, Freddy recognized it was Janie and lowered the pistol. "What are you doing here?"

"Looking for Katy and the kids...um, what are you doing here?" she asked.

"Are you alone?" he called up.

"Yeah, I'm alone," she answered, turning her head toward his voice at the entrance to the basement.

Freddy emerged.

"Where's Ryan?" he asked. "We need him."

"Funny. I was going to ask you to help us."

"Good. We're on the same sheet of music."

"He's at home, securing the house."

Freddy turned to James. "Take the kids back to your house. It's safer there. I'm going to escort Janie home and see if we can't pick up Ryan."

Carbolla's Residence, South Side, Chicago

Antonio threw an already battered and bruised Kaitlyn to the floor.

She winced in pain as she landed on the hardwood planks. She wanted to cry, but for some reason couldn't conjure up the tears. Once more she was someone's captive.

How could this be? She hardened her mind and, like before, planned on escaping.

"If you wanted her dead, then why bring her here?" Rodrigo asked as he looked down at Kaitlyn for a second time that day.

Anthony hadn't thought it through. He knew what he wanted in prison. He knew that he hated Freddy Becker, but now that he had the power of life and death in his hands, something felt different. Was it weakness? Was it empathy? Humanity? He didn't know. He had never killed a person in the *real* world, only in prison. The big house was different – more feral. He looked down upon the broken and beaten woman. He stood tall over her. He puffed out his chest and tried his best to look intimidating and threatening.

She wouldn't look at him. It wasn't that she had surrendered to her fate, it was that she wasn't going to play their game.

"I had him," Antonio answered. "I had him and the GDs interfered. They took Becker, an old man, and the kids. They sent her away. That's how I caught her."

"She must have paid their toll," Rodrigo said. "She has a pass now."

"I don't know what they did with Becker. If he's alive, he may come looking for her. If not, I have no use for her," Antonio said.

"So what's your plan? You just gonna hide in here? You just gonna keep her tucked away for some kind of revenge thing?" Rodrigo asked.

"I haven't decided yet."

"Think on it. You have until morning," Rodrigo said, and walked off.

Antonio looked down at Kaitlyn and sneered.

She still wasn't paying him any attention.

He walked up to her and pulled a pistol from his waistband. He placed the muzzle against her forehead and said, "I should blow your head off, then hang you from an overpass for your husband to find."

Angry, she spit at him.

Fury washed over him. He recoiled back and struck her in the head with the butt of the pistol.

She fell unconscious to the floor.

Pettigrew Residence, Chicago

"Honey, where's the other box of nails?" Ryan called out. A minute passed without hearing a response. Curious as to where she might be, he went looking for her. "Janie, where are you?" He went from room to room, but she wasn't there. Entering the children's room, he opened the door and checked on each of them. "Have either of you seen Mom?" he asked, trying not to raise their fear.

They shook their heads, *no*.

He stooped down next to them. "Listen, I have to leave the house for just a little bit. I need you guys to stay in this room and keep the door shut. Do you understand?"

They nodded.

He kissed them on their foreheads and made one more tour of the house.

Nothing.

It was like she disappeared. The front door was boarded shut, so that left the back door as the only access point. Unsure if something bad had happened, he got his police utility belt from the closet, strapped it on, and pulled his service pistol from the holster. Tactically he cleared the rest of the house and found it empty. *Where could she be?* His concern grew. If she wasn't inside, she must be outside. He exited the house and searched the backyard but still couldn't find her.

With no trace of Janie, Ryan's fear expanded to almost panic. He searched his thoughts for where she could be and came back with the last conversation they'd had concerning the Beckers. *Did she go to see them?* It was the only thing that made sense. Now filled with anger and worry that the Beckers could find out his role in Freddy's arrest and conviction, he started to fill with panic.

He ran to his room and pulled an FN SCAR from his closet. The 7.62 mm semiautomatic rifle resembled an oversized AR-15, but with more kick and stopping power. It was more than enough to kill any man who was to come between him and his search for Janie. He shoved a fully loaded magazine into the magazine well and pulled the charging handle back, which loaded a round into the chamber.

Ready to find Janie and take on anyone, including the

Beckers if they got in his way, he walked out the back door in search of Janie.

Chicago

As Freddy and Janie used the cover of darkness to move, he couldn't shake the nagging question that had plagued him since his arrest, and that was, why had Ryan suddenly been transferred?

"The street looks clear," Janie said, her head popping out and looking around the corner.

"Hold up."

"I could use a break," she said, leaning her back against the cold brick wall.

"What happened the day I was arrested?" he asked.

"I've been wanting to ask you that same question," she answered.

"What do you mean?"

"Ryan came home from work. Something was different. He just wasn't himself. He said he had a transfer notice and that we needed to pack immediately. When I pressed him, he said it was for protection. He mentioned *witness protection.*"

"Did he ever mention protection from what?"

"I just assumed it had to do with those gang members."

"Remember the cookout?"

"Yeah."

"That was all about giving Ryan some time to defuse a little bit. You know, a means to get his mind off the stresses of the job. I know he did have some threats come in. I suppose he mentioned it to the chief, and they acted on it."

"Well, why wouldn't he want you to know?"

The question struck a chord with Freddy. *Why wouldn't he want me to know? What's he hiding? We're best friends!* Freddy dismissed the notion that Ryan was keeping secrets from him. "I don't know, but I'm sure it's nothing. I'm sure he didn't want to feel incriminated alongside me, so he never talked to me again."

"I asked him to go see you, and he wouldn't. I'm sorry about that."

"It's fine, that's all water under the bridge, but now I need him. They have Katy, and I need him 'cause we're going to be outnumbered for sure."

"Wait a second," Janie demanded. "Outnumbered?"

"I don't think De LaRosa is acting alone. Surely, he's had some assistance from the outside. He was incarcerated. I know this because I arrested him. That means somebody from the outside world has acted on his behalf. Maybe a deal or something, I don't know."

"I normally don't want Ryan caught up in anything dangerous, but you all are like family."

"Thank you."

"Just know that Ryan's not acting like himself."

It was yet another comment that gave Freddy pause. *Not himself?* He quickly brushed it off. "Let's keep moving."

"HOW MUCH FURTHER?" Freddy asked, his eyes scanning the street ahead as best he could.

"Not far now. Just up there."

"This is a nice part of town. You not only moved but moved up," Freddy joked.

The sounds of the streets and the violence that was still raging around the city could be heard in all directions.

"Thank God we're not far now. I was beginning to think this wasn't a good idea," Janie said.

The two stepped out and rushed down the street.

Out of the corner of his eye, Freddy saw a beam of light from a flashlight streak over them. "Get down." He shoved Janie to the ground, and the two crawled behind an abandoned car.

"JANIE, IS THAT YOU?" a voice boomed.

"It's Ryan!" Janie exclaimed, jumping to her feet. "Over here."

"That was pure luck," Freddy quipped.

"Why are you out here?" he asked, his tone agitated. "Don't ever do that, you understand me?"

"I'm not a child. Don't reprimand me like one," she scoffed. "I told you. We need help. We can't do this on our own. Besides, Freddy needs us, too."

Freddy stood up from behind the car and waved. "Hi, old friend."

Ryan felt a sudden flush of blood rushing through his ears. His legs grew weak. "What the hell are you doing here?"

"People keep asking me that very same question," Freddy joked.

"I don't know what you want, but you're a convicted murderer and now apparently an escaped felon; we can't be associating with you," Ryan said firmly. "Janie, come; we're headed home."

"Ryan, he needs our help. Katy has been taken," Janie snapped.

Freddy couldn't help but feel hurt by Ryan's initial response, but then again, he was what Ryan said, regardless if he was innocent.

"Who has her?" Ryan asked.

"How about we discuss it at your house?" Freddy said, cautiously looking around.

Gunfire cracked in the distance.

"Good idea," Ryan said. He turned and started the short trek back home with Freddy and Janie in tow.

Carbolla's Residence, South Side, Chicago

"You need to make a decision, now," Rodrigo barked at Antonio.

"All you do is bitch," Antonio spat back.

"I didn't want and still don't want anything to do with this."

"You gave me until morning," Antonio countered.

"That was until she started to scream nonstop. C'mon, just let the bitch go."

"No."

Angered, Rodrigo got into Antonio's face. His nose was less than an inch away. "Then go shut her up. I want to get some sleep."

Gritting his teeth, Antonio snarled, then turned and went back to the bedroom where he held Kaitlyn. He threw the door open and yelled, "Shut up!"

"Go to hell!" Kaitlyn fired back. She was weary of the endless torture she'd received, and even though she thought of escaping, her patience with all of it had reached its peak.

Antonio stepped into the room, swung back and struck her with the back of his hand.

The blow toppled Kaitlyn, but she quickly recovered. "Is that all you have? Huh? My husband was right. You're a weak and pathetic little man."

Not holding back, Antonio clenched his fist, cocked it back, and slammed it against the side of her face.

This blow fazed her, and it took Kaitlyn more than a minute to get off the floor. She wiped the blood that now flowed from her mouth with her hand and laughed. "You really are pathetic."

His anger turning to fury, Antonio cocked his arm back again, but before he could swing, Kaitlyn lashed out and jabbed him in the left thigh with a wire hanger she'd found and fabricated into a weapon.

Shocked by her counterattack, Antonio let out a grunt of pain.

Kaitlyn swung again, and again struck him in the leg. Her confidence built with each strike. She got to her feet and coiled back to slam the hanger into his neck when Rodrigo appeared in the doorway, a pistol in his hand.

She exchanged her last glance with Rodrigo, who promptly pulled the trigger.

Kaitlyn dropped to her knees and fell over dead.

Not expecting Rodrigo to appear, much less the fire of a gun, Antonio scurried away. With eyes wide, he looked at the blood pool around Kaitlyn's head.

"Yo," Rodrigo said.

Antonio looked and now saw the muzzle pointed at him. He defensively raised his hands and said, "No, don't."

"You gonna do as I say going forward?"

"Yes."

Rodrigo shoved the pistol into his waistband and ordered, "Get her body out of here, and clean up the mess."

11

DECEMBER 7, 2014
SOUTH SIDE, CHICAGO

AFTER EXPLAINING everything to Ryan and together concocting a sound plan, the two of them headed out. Janie had volunteered to come, but Ryan wouldn't allow it. Going back to get James was out of the question; plus Freddy wanted him to stay and protect the kids. It would just be the two of them, and together they felt they could do the job, especially since they'd had so much training over the years and because they would have the element of surprise.

As they navigated the streets, the now risen moon helped them see. Block by block they went, each covering the other until they were outside Rodrigo's house.

"So we're just going to go in blasting?" Ryan asked.

"Yep."

"You remember we're cops...I mean, I'm still a cop," Ryan said.

"Listen, when we're done with all of this, you and I need to have a chat about what happened."

Ryan stared off without giving a reply.

The front door of the house stood in between two large windows. A faint glow emanated from the window on the right, most likely from a candle or lantern.

"Maybe we should peek into that front window," Ryan said and got up without waiting for a reply.

"Hey, wait," Freddy said and got up to follow.

Ryan reached the window and poked his head up. Lying on a bed was a man; he couldn't see who it was.

His rifle at the ready, Freddy stood behind Ryan. "Anything?"

"Just one person asleep."

"Then you go for him. I'll break left and clear," Freddy said and marched up to the front door.

"Just like that, we're going in?"

"This is our plan, and I don't have any more time to waste. Katy is most likely here, or they know where she is. Time is no longer on my side or hers." He stepped back and drove his right foot into the door near the handle.

As he expected, the door exploded inward.

Freddy, followed by Ryan, rushed in.

Ryan shouted, "Room right." He kicked that door in to find Mendez waking. Not hesitating, Ryan put two rounds into him.

Freddy was in the living room; his flashlight washed over the space. There sitting in a chair was Carlos, who stood up, pistol in hand. Freddy was on him quickly; he slammed the butt of his rifle into the side of his head, knocking Carlos out.

Emerging from the front bedroom, Ryan swept past Freddy just as Rodrigo and Antonio both were coming out of separate back rooms. He put his light on them and shouted, "Drop your weapons!"

Both Rodrigo and Antonio did as they were ordered.

Freddy came up alongside Ryan and spotted Antonio. "There you are, you son of a bitch." He marched over to Antonio, grabbed him by his T-shirt, and dragged him out into the living room. He threw him down on his knees and placed the muzzle of the rifle against his forehead. "Where is she?"

Following suit, Ryan grabbed Rodrigo and pulled him next to Antonio. When he stepped back, his flashlight caught his face. It was then that he recognized him.

"You," Rodrigo spat.

Not paying attention to Rodrigo, Freddy kept threatening Antonio. "Where is she? What have you done with her?"

"I don't know what you're talking about, Agent Becker," Antonio replied spitefully.

"Liar!"

Ryan didn't want the situation to spin out of control, so he took the duct tape he had brought from his pack and used it to secure the three men's arms behind their backs.

Carlos woke as soon as Ryan was done and rolled onto his back. "What the –"

"Just shut up," Ryan barked, his muzzle waving in Carlos's face.

"Don't shoot, man," Carlos begged.

"I'll ask one more time, and then I'm going to shoot you," Freddy growled.

"I don't know what you're talking about," Antonio answered.

Ryan stood back next to Freddy and kept his eyes on Rodrigo, who kept staring at him intently.

Freddy caught the peculiar looks each man was giving him and said, "Does he know something?"

Not answering the question directly, Ryan said, "I'm going to search the house." He stepped off and headed down the hall.

"Do you know where she is?" Freddy asked Rodrigo.

"I don't know who you're talking about," Rodrigo answered.

"Where is she?"

"I told you, *jefe*. I don't know what you're talking about."

A deluge of anger, hate, and rage filled Freddy's mind. His veins burned with adrenaline, and he knew, without a shadow of a doubt, that these men had something to do with Kaitlyn's disappearance. Freddy wanted to kill Rodrigo. He felt he had to show that he was willing to use lethal force to compel them to talk. He placed the muzzle of the rifle on Rodrigo's forehead and barked, "Tell me."

Rodrigo laughed. "You won't shoot me, *jefe*! You're a cop. Cops don't kill."

Freddy got the sense that Rodrigo was the one in charge, so killing him might not be the most advantageous, but still he wanted to let them know he was intent on doing anything to find Kaitlyn.

"You're wrong; I'm not a cop. According to the court, I'm a murderer," he said, pointed the rifle at Carlos, and pulled the trigger.

The single shot from the M4 smashed through Carlos's head, leaving brains and blood splattered on the floor.

"What the hell, man!" Rodrigo howled.

"Now whoever tells me first won't die," Freddy said.

Ryan came running into the room. "Freddy, I found her. I found Katy."

Rodrigo looked over to the doorway where Ryan was standing, and stared at him again. "I know you, don't I?"

Again, the comment caught Freddy off guard. It stopped him in his tracks. He looked at Ryan and asked, "What's he talking about?"

"I arrested him a while back," Ryan answered nervously.

Freddy picked up on Ryan's shift in tone.

"Are you two friends?" Rodrigo snarked. "'Cause I don't think your friend is really your friend."

"Don't listen to him. He's talking trash. Now let me take you to Katy."

Freddy looked over at Rodrigo, who stood erect on his knees, a devilish grin stretched across his face. "How do you know him?"

"I know him from –"

Before Rodrigo could finish his sentence, Ryan lifted his

rifle and put two rounds into his chest, sending him to the floor dead.

That was all Freddy needed to know. "What have you done?"

"I killed a thug," Ryan replied.

"No, what have you done?"

"It's not what you think!"

"I don't know, what am I thinking?" Freddy asked, his spine stiffening.

"I didn't have anything to do with this, not this," Ryan answered with a stutter.

"You...what did you do?"

"It was the only way. The Latin Kings were relentless. They said they wouldn't stop unless I did what they wanted. They offered me a way out, so I took it."

"What did you do?" Freddy again asked, his anger rising fast.

"I framed you. I took your pistol...I killed that gang-banger," Ryan admitted.

"You framed me?" Freddy screamed.

"I'm sorry," Ryan answered. "That was it. I didn't have anything to do with this."

Freddy jumped on top of Ryan and began beating him. Over and over he landed clenched fists into Ryan's face.

Seeing his opportunity, Antonio jumped to his feet and ran out of the house, his arms taped behind his back.

Freddy didn't care. He still wasn't done taking out his anger on Ryan. After a few more powerful blows, Freddy fell off Ryan and crawled to the wall and leaned against it. "How did Katy get mixed up in all of this?"

"I-I don't know," Ryan answered through his bloody lips.

"Where is she?" Freddy asked.

"There's a shed in the backyard," Ryan answered, blood spitting with each word he spoke.

His focus back on finding Kaitlyn, Freddy got to his feet and headed out the back door.

In the left corner of the lot stood a rusty metal utility shed.

Armed with his rifle, now slung, and a flashlight, Freddy walked up to the shed door. "Katy?" he asked, hoping to hear her response. Suddenly fear gripped him. Ryan hadn't said he'd found her alive; he'd just said that he found her.

Freddy tore open the door and flashed his light inside. There on a filthy and bloody blue tarp lay Kaitlyn's lifeless body.

He fell to his knees and reached out for her. "Baby?" He pulled her body close, and by his touch on her cold skin, he knew for sure that she was dead. Unable to hold back his emotions, he erupted into an irreconcilable fit of sorrow. He cradled her in his arms and put his face next to hers, his warm tears splashing down on her ice-cold skin. Lost in despair, he sobbed.

Browning Residence, Chicago

No one bothered Freddy as he slowly marched through the chaotic streets, probably because cradled in his arms was a dead person. The occasional person shouted at him, but no one dared come close. Or maybe because they could sense that Freddy was now a man who didn't care. Buried deeper than his sorrow was a rage; all it would take would be one person doing something and he could go on a killing rampage. The man who once heralded law and order was gone. If someone dared to confront him, he had zero qualms about being judge, jury and executioner.

When he reached James's house, he paused. How would he explain to the kids? He was at a loss, and the simplest thing was to just tell them the truth. He scaled the concrete steps and kicked the door eight times, a signal he and James had agreed to.

The curtains to his right moved, no doubt James peering out.

The door opened, and in the light of the moon James appeared. He looked down, then up at Freddy. "Is she?"

"She's gone."

With a shaking hand, James opened the door and let Freddy in.

"Where are the kids?"

"Asleep downstairs. They're safe," James replied as he closed and locked the door.

"Where should I lay her?" Freddy asked, looking around

the dimly lit room. The only light emanated from two large candles.

"Anywhere, ah, no, how about the guest bedroom," James answered, his voice cracking. He rushed off down the hall. "This way."

Freddy followed; he carefully maneuvered down the narrow hall, trying not to have her head hit the wall. In the room he laid her on the bed. Blood began to flow back into his arms, followed by a tingling sensation.

James sat on the edge of the bed and picked up Kaitlyn's cold hand. He brought it to his lips and kissed it. "My baby girl, I'm so sorry."

"Daddy," a small voice sounded in the darkened doorway.

Freddy turned and ushered Kayleigh back into the hallway, closing the door behind him.

"Was that Mommy?" she asked in her sweet voice.

"It was. Now how about you go back downstairs and go to bed."

"I have to go pee, and Papa said we should probably go outside, but I'm scared."

"It's fine, use the bathroom," Freddy said. He understood what James was trying to do by not using the plumbing, but he no longer planned on staying in Chicago. There wasn't anything there for him, and he needed to get his family to safety.

"Can I go kiss Mommy?" she asked tenderly.

"No, now hurry on, please," Freddy said, fighting back tears.

Kayleigh leaned in and kissed Freddy on the cheek, then recoiled. "Your face is cold."

"Go on," he said and gently turned her in the direction of the bathroom. He watched her as she headed down the hall and disappeared into the bathroom. When the door closed, he fell back against the wall and sobbed. He missed Kaitlyn so much, and talking to the kids was always her strong suit. How would he tell them? Could he console them? He wasn't really the most nurturing type. His pain was only matched by his anger. He knew he needed to leave Chicago, but could he do so with the knowledge that Antonio was still out there? And if they did leave, where would they go?

———

THE SMELL of coffee woke Freddy. He shot up and looked around the room now drenched in warm sunlight. He swung his legs off the couch and set them on the floor. As he stood, he heard voices from the kitchen. He paused for a second to stretch his bruised and sore body. He'd been through a lot over the past couple of days, and at the rate he was going, he'd be a physically broken man in no time.

"He's awake," Kayleigh said, her small head peeking around the corner.

Freddy turned the same corner to find Michael, Kayleigh and James sitting at the small dinette table in the corner of the kitchen.

"I made fresh coffee using a French press. Thank goodness for that little propane stove I had for camping."

For a moment all seemed fine, but it wasn't. Kaitlyn was still dead, and the world had essentially ended.

"Kids, we need to talk," Freddy said as he took a seat at the head of the table.

"Where's Mommy?" Michael asked.

"That's what I want to discuss," Freddy replied, an uneasy expression on his face. He pinched his brow together and thought about how he'd tell them. Was there a certain way you said things?

"Is now a good time?" James asked.

Freddy didn't answer. He shot James a look that said more than words could.

"I'll go get some more coffee," James said, getting up from the table.

His hands shaking, Freddy reached and took a hand from each child into his. He gently squeezed and gave them a tender smile. Just as he was formulating how to say it, Michael blurted out, "She's dead."

Eyes wide with surprise, Freddy stared at Michael.

Kayleigh started to cry.

"Why would you say that?" Freddy asked.

"Because of the way you and Papa are acting and..." Michael said but hesitated from finishing his comment.

"And what?" Freddy asked.

"I saw her...last night."

"You went into the guest bedroom?" James asked, he too

in shock at Michael's comment.

"No, I, um," Michael said, his head hung low. He stared at his fidgeting hands as he was unable to make eye contact with anyone.

"Son, tell me," Freddy said.

"I saw her in a dream. She said she was going to be alright," Michael muttered, his voice now muffled from anguish and tears.

Kayleigh's tears grew in intensity.

Faced with two emotional children, Freddy took a deep breath and said, "Mommy was killed. She's here in the house, and later on we will bury her in the backyard."

Kayleigh jumped up from her seat and into Freddy's arms.

Michael followed suit.

The three embraced, tears all flowing from each.

Not wanting James to feel left out, Freddy looked over and said, "Bring it in here, Papa."

Reluctant at first, James relented and joined the three.

Michael pulled away and asked, "Can I see her?"

"Not a good idea," Freddy said, knowing her condition wasn't good.

"It's fine," James said. "After you went to bed, I cleaned her up and put her into one of Nana's dresses. You know the two were always swapping clothes."

"You really want to see her?" Freddy asked Michael, who nodded in return. "And what about you?" he asked Kayleigh.

She too nodded.

"Then let's go see Mommy," Freddy said, getting up from his seat, each child clinging to him still.

De LaRosa Residence, South Side, Chicago

Using his teeth to tear the bandage, Antonio wrapped the puncture wounds he'd received from the hanger Kaitlyn jabbed him with.

When he finished, he tossed the gauze aside and opened a bottle of tequila he had stashed away in the cupboards of his mother's house. He could still smell her scent as if she were just in the other room. The lavender perfume she wore had now become a part of the old house along with everything else. It was something he never thought he'd find comfort in, yet here he was at peace.

His mind repeatedly went over the details of the night before. He'd accomplished everything he had wanted to, but something felt wrong. All he had wanted was for Freddy to know the pain he'd suffered through, yet he felt as if something was off or, better yet, that the job wasn't done.

Should he now find Freddy and kill him? Was that the next organic progression of their feud? He didn't doubt that Freddy would come for him; heck, he would, and he didn't think he and Freddy were all that different.

Knowing that he was a target of a man who would no doubt be relentless, he figured that the best strategy would be to go on the offense. He knew where he lived, so why not go there and finish this once and for all?

Browning Residence, Chicago

Lost in despair and in his troubled thoughts, Freddy barely heard James recite Kaitlyn's favorite Bible verse or the children crying incessantly. Finally, the three left and he was alone, towering over the open gravesite, Kaitlyn's body wrapped in a decorative duvet cover.

James returned and placed a gentle hand on Freddy's shoulder. "You've been quiet."

"There's nothing to say."

"The kids are downstairs; I think you need to go talk to them again."

"There's nothing to say," Freddy repeated.

"Son, I know this pain. I lost –"

Agitated, Freddy shrugged James's hand off his shoulder and turned to face him. "You don't know how this feels."

"You're upset. You have to remember that I also lost a child," James reminded him.

Freddy paused before he put his foot in his mouth. James was right, he suddenly thought. All of them had lost, and all were suffering immeasurably.

"Listen, we need to figure out what we're going to do," James said. "We can't stay here; we need to leave the city."

"And how do we do that?"

"Walk if we have to, but we need to leave. Things will only get worse," James said.

Freddy thought about it. Again, James was right. "Where are we going to go?"

"I've got an old friend. We're like brothers, have been for fifty years. He lives in the Ozarks; he has a large swath of land."

"And he'll let us stay with him?"

"Yes."

Freddy turned away and began to pace the yard.

"What's on your mind, son?"

"I can't leave, not yet. There's unfinished business."

"Fritz, don't be a damn fool. We need to leave and do so as quickly as we can."

"I can't."

"And what exactly do you have to finish?"

"I have to find him, I must. He needs to pay for what he did."

"And who's that?"

"De LaRosa. He killed Katy, and I aim to kill him."

James walked up to Freddy and sighed.

"Take the kids; head south to your friend's house. I'll meet you later."

"No."

"Yes."

"No!"

"Now look who's being stubborn," Freddy quipped.

"This isn't funny. You're about to go risk your life, and for what, some distorted sense of justice? Your place is with these kids."

"I have to do this," Freddy said, giving James one last look before walking off.

12

DECEMBER 8, 2014

DE LAROSA RESIDENCE, SOUTH SIDE, CHICAGO

ANXIETY COURSED through Antonio's body. Like Freddy, he had now become obsessed with killing the other, but this time he wanted an assurance and a real plan of attack. For him to have that, he needed men, and it took him a full day to gather those Latin Kings willing to work with him.

By the time the previous day had turned to night, he had three others who were willing to help his cause, not out of an allegiance to him, but for Rodrigo.

Rodrigo might have been one of the Latin Kings' main street enforcers, but he was widely liked and respected. These men had no families and, upon hearing the story of how Rodrigo was murdered, aimed to get revenge.

After getting three men – Julio, Jose and Juan; all brothers – Antonio had dispatched Julio to gather intelligence on Freddy by casing his property.

"Where's Julio?" Antonio asked, his frustration and impatience displayed in his tone.

"Chill, he's what you call a very detail-oriented person. He will be back soon," Juan replied. He played with a sheath knife he'd recently looted from an REI store in midtown. Juan was the oldest, with Julio being the youngest. All looked remarkably similar, with dark hair kept long on top and cropped tight on the sides. Tattoos covered their bodies, including a few on their faces. They each had a medium build, and none would be called physical specimens, but all were known to be fierce and brutal street fighters.

"You really need to chill, homie," Jose said, chuckling. "You're making me nervous."

"I need this to go right this time," Antonio barked back.

"Listen, we don't really know you, and don't think for a second you're in charge. We're not doing this for you, we're doing this for Rodrigo. Now stop acting like you're some sort of boss, 'cause you ain't," Juan snapped back.

"Do you want to kill the man who killed Rodrigo, huh?"

"We're here, aren't we?" Juan replied.

"Then you'll do as I say. This man we're after, he's trained, he's smart, and the last time I ran into him, he had backup. We need to be smart."

Juan leapt to his feet and marched over to Antonio. With his chest puffed out, he got within inches of Antonio's face. "I will do what I want to do. You don't snap your fingers and tell the Ramirez brothers what to do, you get me?"

Antonio opened his mouth to reply when the front door opening interrupted him.

"He's leaving," Julio said, breathing heavily.

"Then we need to go now," Juan said.

"Is anyone else with him?" Antonio asked.

"Just some old man and two kids. They're packing up stuff into a wagon. I saw them coming and going from his house to another a block away."

"You didn't see another guy, about his age?" Antonio asked.

"No, just him, some old man and two kids, no one else. They're taking stuff from his house to the other house. I think that's where the old man lives," Julio answered. He walked over and sat down in a chair, sweat dripping off his brow.

"Sounds like your boy is packing up to leave town. Now's the time to get him," Juan said.

"Well?" Jose asked, he too now standing tall, chest out.

Antonio paced.

"Screw you. We're going. We don't need you," Juan said, motioning to his brothers.

"Wait," Antonio said.

"Now what?" Jose asked.

"We're not just going to kill Becker, we're going to kill all of them," Antonio said.

"The kids too?" Julio asked. "They're, like, little ones."

"All of them," Antonio replied.

"I don't care. We take them all out," Juan said.

Jose shrugged his shoulders, acknowledging his lack of concern.

"Now that everyone agrees, let's go," Antonio said.

Pettigrew Residence, Chicago

Janie followed Ryan into the bedroom. This time she wouldn't take no for an answer. "You need to tell me now, what happened?"

"I told you that I don't want to talk about it," Ryan said, shoving more clothes into a backpack.

"Did you find Katy?"

Frustrated, Ryan decided to lie. He dropped what he was doing, faced her and said, "We went to the house. We found Katy; she was dead. Then things went bad, and Fritz was killed. I barely made it out of there with my life."

Finally hearing something that made sense as to why Ryan had been acting scared, her displeasure with him melted away. She stepped towards him and put her arms over his shoulders. "Why didn't you just tell me?"

"I was going to...um, I just didn't know how to say it. I didn't want you upset."

Tears formed in her eyes.

He returned her embrace. "I love you, Janie. I hope you know that."

"I know you do, and I know you'll do anything to keep us safe."

He pulled away and looked into her eyes. "Thank you for saying that."

"I'll go finish packing the food in the kitchen," she said.

"Good 'cause I want to be heading out by daybreak."

She stopped at the door to the bedroom, turned and asked, "Should we go find the Becker kids and take them with us?"

"Janie, we need to just head south towards your mother's house in Decatur and don't look back."

"But maybe we could think about taking them with us?"

"They have their grandfather; they'll be fine."

"But –"

"Janie, enough!" he snapped.

Not wishing to argue with him again, she turned and left the room.

He let out a heavy sigh. He hated being in the situation he was in, and he hated to lie. It ran counter to his core beliefs, yet there he was telling another lie. If he could just get his family out of town, he could literally close this chapter of his life for good and hopefully never have to think about it again.

Browning Residence, Chicago

Along with Freddy, James was busy packing and organizing their gear and food stores for what promised to be a long and slow march south to Lake of the Ozarks.

His years of preparedness had paid off, as he had years of dehydrated food stores in sealed containers. While it would require water to reconstitute, the containers were easy to pack in the wagons, and they'd have enough food to get them where they were going and then some.

He had given up on talking with Freddy about not going out to seek revenge, as each time he tried, he found resistance.

He proudly looked at the two wagons, both packed, that they'd haul on their way south. It wasn't the most ideal situation, but as he liked to say, "It is what it is."

Crying came from the kitchen.

Concerned, James raced down the hall and into the kitchen, to discover Kayleigh whimpering, her face in her hands.

Standing at the counter was Freddy, his arms crossed, and a look of pain contorted his face.

"What happened?" James asked, going to Kayleigh without giving a second's thought about Freddy.

"I told her that I have to leave," Freddy answered.

"I assume you told her why?"

"Of course not."

Angered, James finally decided to let Freddy have it. "You're a stupid man, you know that? Your daughter has lost her mother, and now she's facing the fact that she may lose you, and for what? Your honor or some distorted code that justice has to be served? Really? Do you care about these kids at all?"

"That's not fair, and of course I care about them," Freddy countered.

"If you truly cared, you'd stay and leave with us in the morning."

"I told you, I have to do this."

"You don't have to do anything. You are choosing to do this. When they had Katy, you did have to go, but now you don't have to leave. Everything that should mean something is in this house right now; it's not out there."

"You'll never understand," Freddy flippantly said.

Standing tall, his body shaking with anger, James barked, "You're right, Fritz, I don't understand. I'll never understand how a man could walk out that door and risk never coming home, all for some sort of code. You're never going to clear your name, and even if you did, does it even matter now? I don't think the world cares about your name being restored to honor; I think the world is dealing with just surviving now. Giving a hoot about your name and honor only speaks to your selfishness. What about their lives?"

"How dare you accuse me of not caring about my children's lives. I'd do anything –"

"Anything? Anything except staying here with your children. You're leaving them with me, an old man. If something happens to you on this crusade of justice, then what? What happens to them? Think, man, think clearly, but don't you ever say you'll do anything, 'cause your leaving puts them in greater danger than staying."

Frustrated by the accusations and that once more James's wisdom rang true, he darted out of the kitchen and towards the front door.

"Where are you going? Running away again?" James barked.

Freddy stopped, spun around and said, "If you weren't my kin, I'd –"

"Daddy, stop, please," Kayleigh cried out.

With a clenched fist, Freddy punched the wall – his pride screamed for an outlet. He grunted in pain and anger, then turned back towards the front door and exited the house.

JAMES GAVE Freddy an hour to cool off before he went out to talk to him again. He opened the door, and there sitting on the front steps was Freddy, his head in his hands.

"Son, care if I sit down next to you?" James asked.

"Sure."

Using the railing for support, James lowered himself to the step and sat. "I'd like to talk to you again."

"You were right," Freddy blurted out.

"I suppose a broken clock is right twice a day, huh?"

"You were. I needed someone to truly tell it to me straight, and you did."

"Then you're not leaving?"

"No."

"Good. Now that that's settled, we should think about heading out at first light," James said.

"Agreed."

James patted Freddy on the back.

"Thanks again, I know I can be stubborn…"

"And stupid," James quipped.

"That too, ha," Freddy said. "Katy was my anchor and compass. She kept me grounded and always could lead me in the right direction. I'm going to really miss her."

"Me too."

Sounds of gunfire cracked in the distance, causing both men to look up.

"So you think this is more than just the city?" James asked.

"Yeah, I'm suspecting, because where's the National Guard? Now this could be regional, meaning other parts of the country are doing fine, but either way, we're screwed here, and we need to get out of here."

Freddy's words were music to James's ears.

"I suppose I'd better go in and apologize," Freddy said, the pain clearly visible in his expression.

James looked intently at Freddy's lean and chiseled face, a solid stubble now covering the lower half. "Son, we can get through this."

"I know, and I'm grateful to God you're here," Freddy said. "Thanks, Dad."

"You're welcome, son."

The front door opened suddenly.

The two men looked back and saw Kayleigh standing there. "I'm hungry."

With a broad smile, Freddy said, "Let's get you something to eat, then."

"Hey, Agent Becker!" a voice boomed from across the street.

Freddy spun around to see Antonio emerging from behind a car, pistol out in front of him.

"Quick, get inside," Freddy ordered. He helped James to his feet. Freddy looked again and now saw more men had emerged; they too had pistols.

Not a second passed before bullets began to strike the front of the house.

Freddy scooped up Kayleigh, and the two leapt through the open front door. With his leg, Freddy kicked the door closed. He unwrapped his arms and set Kayleigh on the floor then pulled his pistol from his waistband and went to the window next to the door. He pulled the drape aside and spotted Antonio still standing in the street. He was pointing in a different direction and giving orders in Spanish.

"James, get the kids down in the basement and come back with your rifle!" Freddy hollered.

One step ahead of him, James came in the front room, rifle in hand. He called out to Kayleigh, "Get downstairs, sweetie."

Kayleigh didn't move.

"Sweetie?" James asked and stepped towards the little girl still lying on the floor. He stood over her and saw a large red spot growing on her tan shirt. Dropping to his knees, he examined her, to find she wasn't breathing. "Fritz!"

"C'mon, you bastards," Freddy barked at Antonio and the

others, who were still out front, no doubt deliberating how to attack.

"Fritz!" James yelled, his voice panicked.

Freddy looked over and quickly saw what James had. Kayleigh was down, not moving, and there was now a pool of blood forming around her back. "No, no, no!" He raced to Kayleigh's side, dropped to his knees, and scooped her up. "No, this can't be happening." He placed his ear against her chest to listen but heard nothing. Using two fingers, he checked for a pulse, but still nothing. "No!"

Heavy footsteps sounded just outside the front door.

"They're here," James called out, raising his rifle and flipping the selector switch to SEMI.

"Baby, wake up, wake up!" Freddy howled in agony.

Kayleigh was gone. A bullet had struck her in the chest, passed through her heart, and exited her back.

The door exploded in.

Quick to act, James let several rounds loose, striking Julio squarely in the chest. He hobbled back and fell off the front steps and onto the sidewalk. He clutched his chest and gargled up blood.

Antonio, Juan, and Jose simultaneously advanced on the open front door.

The gunfire snapped Freddy from the shock of what had just happened. He picked up his pistol, which he'd laid next to Kayleigh, stood, and fired one well-aimed shot at Juan.

Juan crumpled to the ground like a heavy sack. His body lay twitching on the cold sidewalk.

Not showing a concern for anything, including his own safety, Freddy exited the house, pistol out in front of him. He took aim on Jose and fired, striking him in the chest. He fired again; once more the round hit Jose perfectly in the center of his chest.

Much like Juan, Jose toppled over dead.

Antonio pulled the trigger of his pistol numerous times, but each round missed Freddy, with one getting as close as punching through a loose part of his jeans and hitting the doorjamb behind Freddy.

Pivoting, Freddy aimed at Antonio.

Scared for his life, Antonio took off running down the street.

Freddy took pursuit.

Dumbfounded at how his plan had failed, Antonio cursed at himself loudly. He had gone there with superior numbers and the element of surprise, but now he was the man being hunted.

Freddy ran the fastest his legs would take him.

On the other hand, Antonio was having a hard time. One leg was sore from being stabbed by Kaitlyn, and he just wasn't in as good a shape as he thought he was. He knew the only way to get away would be to hide somewhere. He turned right and darted down an alleyway, hurdled a short fence, and burst through a half-open side door of a house.

Screams from the occupants echoed into the street.

Freddy wasn't far behind. He too hurdled the fence and darted into the house; however, he wouldn't make it out, as he was clotheslined by someone. He slammed into the floor, smacking his head hard.

Antonio exploded out the front door and back onto the street. He looked back to see if Freddy was pursuing him, but saw no one; however, he wasn't about to declare victory.

He made a hard left then another and sprinted down the street as best he could until he was blocks away. He stopped, took cover behind an abandoned car, his heart beating heavily and sweat dripping off his brow and down his back.

"C'mon, you son of a bitch." His eyes were glued on the street, expecting to see Becker, but he was nowhere to be seen. After a few minutes, he left his hiding spot and took off back down the street towards his mother's house.

"WHAT THE HELL are you doing here, Fritz?" a large burly man asked, picking Freddy off the floor.

"How long have I been out?" Freddy asked, his head still swooning from the hard fall.

"A minute or two at the most," the man said. His name was Max, and he was a friendly neighbor who had known the Beckers for years.

Freddy shook off the fall. "Sorry, I was in pursuit. Any idea where he went?"

"Out the front door. I'd have stopped him, but he was too fast. You, on the other hand."

Freddy shoved the pistol back into his waistband and marched towards the front door. "See ya, Max."

"Say, Fritz, what do you make of all this?"

"It's not good."

"Should we be doing something?"

Freddy stopped at the front door, turned back and replied, "Yeah, getting the hell out of Chicago."

WHEN FREDDY ARRIVED BACK HOME, he not only found Kayleigh dead, but James had been shot too, a fact that James hadn't revealed. Then again, there was so much chaos happening, and Freddy had made pursuit rapidly without checking on James.

"I was wrong," James said as he coughed up blood.

"How?" Freddy asked as he cleaned the wound, to find the bullet hadn't exited.

"If you had gone out to kill those bastards, our little Kayleigh would still be here," James said as he grunted in pain.

"Dad, I'm going to have to try to get the bullet out," Freddy said.

"Ah, shit," James cursed. He wasn't known to do so, but now seemed like an appropriate time.

"If I don't, the wound will fester."

"Hold on."

"Yeah."

"You know where that son of a bitch lives, don't you?" James asked.

"Yeah."

"Then go get him...now."

"I can't. I've got to try to get the bullet out."

James took hold of Freddy's arm and squeezed. "Go now."

"No, that train has left the station. I have to take care of Michael and you."

"That man is now responsible for killing my daughter and grandbaby. He deserves death."

"Dad, I know what he deserves, but what if something happened to me? I can't risk that, and if I don't get this bullet out, you'll die too."

"You're too darn stubborn."

"First you wanted me to stay; now you want me to go. Listen, Dad, I'm not going."

"Like I said, I was wrong."

"It doesn't matter anymore."

"What are you doing over there?" James asked Michael, who hovered in the open doorway.

"Son, you're not going to want to be here."

"Can I help?" Michael asked.

"Not a good idea," Freddy replied.

"Let the boy help. This is a new world now, and he'll need to know how to do this sort of stuff. No sense coddling the boy."

Freddy nodded and said, "Go get me some water and clean towels."

"Okay," Michael said and took off at a quick pace.

"He's a good boy," James said. Again he coughed. Blood now covered his lips. He wiped them and looked at his hand. "That can't be good."

"It's not," Freddy said. He wasn't a surgeon, much less knew enough to operate on a human, but what he did know was that if he couldn't get the bullet out, James would most certainly die. Then an idea came to mind. Janie was a nurse practitioner. The chance was there that she could help. "Dad, I've got an idea, but it requires that I go get Janie."

"What's this idea?"

"I'm not a doctor, but Janie, she has a medical background. I think I should go get her."

James nodded.

Michael entered the room, with a large bowl full of water, and clean towels tucked under his arm. "Here, Dad."

"Set it over there," Freddy said.

Michael did as he was asked. "Now what?"

"Now you're going to watch over Papa until I return. I need to go get Mrs. Pettigrew. She'll be able to help me with Papa."

Concern spread over Michael's face. "You're leaving...again?"

"Only because I have to."

Michael turned his fearful gaze towards James.

"It'll be fine. He needs to go," James assured him.

Freddy walked up to Michael, pulled out his pistol, and handed it to Michael. "If anyone comes into the house, you shoot them. Pull the trigger until they fall to the floor. You got it?"

Michael nervously looked at the pistol in his small hand. "I can do it."

Tousling his hair, Freddy said, "Good boy. Love you, son."

Returning his look, Michael replied, "Love you too, Dad."

Pettigrew Residence, Chicago

Much like Freddy, the Pettigrews had packed their belongings and gear into a wagon and the rest into backpacks. With no vehicles, they had to do what no doubt many were doing, hike out of the city.

Janie stepped into the garage, the glow of the lantern casting her shadow on the walls. She smiled at Ryan taking inventory. "Will we be ready?"

"We will, but I wish I had more. How are we looking for food?"

"Enough for a week, max," she replied.

"We need to find more. Maybe I should try to go out and scavenge," he said, his furrowed brow indicating to Janie how nervous he was about their situation.

"We'll find some once we get out of the city," she said.

"Maybe."

"What do you suppose we'll find out past the city limits?" Janie asked.

"I don't know."

She grew silent, her head pivoted down. "What's happened to us?"

He gave her a concerned look. "What do you mean?"

"Not us, like you and me, but us as society?"

"It appears we weren't as united as we thought."

"Will it be like this in the country too?"

"I'm sure it's a bit like this everywhere. This is more about human nature versus location When people get scared, they do things...they act differently, you know, in their own interest." He couldn't help but think of his own actions in regard to Freddy.

"Well, I hope I never do that. I'm a nurse, a healthcare provider, and I'll always make myself available to help those in need."

"Don't be so quick to make a judgment call. How will you act if we don't find food in a week and you have to look at the boys and explain why we weren't prepared?"

"We will be fine. We just need to get out of the city. Plus, I'm sure the government will come soon to help."

"Are you so sure of that?"

"Why, do you really think this is that bad?"

"Look around, the city is tearing itself apart. Where are the police, the firefighters, the National Guard? There's no one. I think this is very, very bad. We need to start thinking differently."

"If you're suggesting that the world has come to an end, that's crazy. This can't be that bad," Janie said. She couldn't imagine everything had fallen apart, and kept clinging to the false notion that what had happened was merely in the city.

"If we come upon food, I'm taking it," Ryan said.

"Of course," she said.

"Even if I have to steal it."

"Now you're talking about stealing. What's gotten into you?"

"I'll do what's necessary to save my family, and I won't risk my life foolishly."

"Not true. Look at how you responded when Becker came. I know you two had a falling-out, but when he came calling, you helped," she said, taking Ryan's hand and squeezing it tenderly.

He couldn't look her in the eyes; his conscience was eating him alive. "I suppose that's what friends do for each other."

"They were like family; I'm going to miss them."

"Me too."

"Can I convince you to stop by their house, check on the kids on our way out of town?" she asked.

He jerked his hand away. "No. I told you. No stops. We're headed out of town and leaving this place to a bad memory, nothing more."

"What's wrong with you? You go from talking fondly of them, like they're family, and now you can't go out of your way a couple of blocks to check on their kids?"

He stepped over to the wagon and fiddled with a strap. "Are the kids asleep?"

"Yes."

"Good. I think it's time for you to get some rest too," Ryan said, not looking at her.

Banging on the door startled them both.

Ryan grabbed a pistol that he had sitting on a bench and headed into the darkened house.

Janie was close behind him.

More banging came from the front door.

"Who do you think it is?" Janie whispered.

His pistol firmly in his grip, Ryan advanced towards the door.

"Ryan, open up," Freddy hollered.

"Is that –?"

"Be quiet," Ryan snapped. He maneuvered up to the front door and stopped to the left of it, his back against the wall.

Janie approached the door.

"What are you doing?" Ryan asked urgently.

"I'm letting our dead friend inside," she mocked. She threw the deadbolt, unlocked the door, and opened it. "Freddy, hey."

Not bothering to come in, Freddy said, "Janie, I need you. It's urgent."

"Come inside."

"No, it's James. He's been shot."

Janie grabbed a coat near her and stepped outside.

Ryan appeared in the door.

The two men glanced at each other but didn't say a word.

Janie faced Ryan and said, "You and I will need to have a heart-to-heart when I return."

"You can't go."

"You heard him. They need me."

"No, he's, um, he's up to no good," Ryan said, his voice cracking.

"Up to no good? You said he was dead?"

"He wishes I were dead," Freddy said.

"You can't go. I forbid it," Ryan snapped.

"I'm going, but you need to stay here with the kids."

"We're all coming with you," Ryan said and ran off to wake the boys.

"Wait, Ryan, why are you doing that?" Janie asked. She faced Freddy and asked, "Can you tell me what's going on?"

"I'll give you the condensed version. "Katy and Kayleigh are dead, and James has been shot...oh, and Ryan had me framed for murder."

Shocked by the news, Janie gave him a puzzled look. "Wait, Katy and Kayleigh are dead?"

"We really don't have much time," Freddy urged. "I need your expertise. James has a bullet lodged in him."

Ryan emerged from the shadows with Randy and Ricky in tow.

"I'm tired," Ricky moaned.

"Where are we going?" Randy asked, rubbing the sleep from his eyes.

"This is foolish," Janie said, her hands on her hips.

"We're going with you, and that's that," Ryan said.

"Ry, just so you know. I'm over it," Freddy said, turned and walked off the front steps and back to the street.

"You really need to tell me what's going on between you two after this is over. And what does he mean that you framed him?"

"It's a long story," Ryan said, following her outside, with the kids just behind him.

"We'll have plenty of time soon enough, and I expect a straight answer," Janie said.

Browning Residence, Chicago

Upon arriving at the house, they found James dead. He'd bled out in the time it took for Freddy to leave and return.

"I'm really sorry for your losses," Janie said, her arm draped over Freddy's shoulder.

"It's becoming commonplace," Freddy said. He stood staring at James's body; the sheets were soaked with blood. "My world is falling apart."

"What can we do to help?" Janie asked.

"You can help me bury him and Kayleigh," he said.

"Of course. Just know that we're here for you and Michael. If you need anything, we'll do our best."

A thought popped into Freddy's mind. "You really want to help?"

"Yes."

"Then watch over Michael as Ryan and I go finish this."

"Finish what?" she asked.

"I'm going to go kill the man who killed my family."

"Do you think that's wise?"

"No, but it's the right thing to do, and sometimes they don't align."

Janie rubbed his arm and let the moment marinate for a few seconds. "Killing this man. Will it bring you peace?"

"Yes," he replied without hesitation. He'd come a long way since being a cop. He had been a man whose life revolved around the concept of law and order. There were laws, and people were given due process, but now those ideals seemed obsolete, or had the world changed to the point that law and order meant something else? By killing Antonio, he was attempting in his own way to bring order to what had become a lawless place. By removing a vile man, he could be saving another life. He liked that definition and went with it.

"Are you okay? You seem lost in thought," she said.

"No, Janie, I'm not okay, but as soon as I kill Antonio De LaRosa, I will be."

"Then go do it. I'll convince Ryan to go with you," Janie said.

The two left the back bedroom where James had been. They found Ryan in the kitchen, sitting down at the dinette table, playing with the wick of a lit candle. Seeing Freddy, Ryan pointed at the wagon in the kitchen and said, "We're using one of those silly wagons too. I'm glad I didn't sell the damn thing on Craigslist now. And, boy, you're stocked up. Is your father-in-law a prepper or something?"

Janie cut him a hard look.

"Will he be fine?" Ryan asked, picking up on the cue from Janie.

"He's gone," Freddy answered.

"Sorry."

"Ryan, I need you to go with Freddy," Janie said, her arms folded and her back arched. She stood with confidence and defiance.

"Go where?"

"To help me kill De LaRosa."

"I already helped you before," Ryan whined.

"You owe me," Freddy said.

"I agree with him. What you did, that wasn't right."

"I did it for us, to protect us. I didn't have a choice," Ryan said defensively.

"I told you, it doesn't matter anymore. All I care about is avenging the deaths of my family."

"And what about avenging the man who helped frame you?" Ryan asked.

"I'm past that. Will you come with me or not?"

"No."

"Ryan Pettigrew, you're going with him!" Janie fired back.

"No, I'm not. I vowed to protect my family. Running off to possibly get killed doesn't do that. I won't go."

"You will," Janie insisted.

"I love you, but I won't. I'll stay here, I'll watch over Michael, but that's it. When you return, we'll say our good-byes, and that's it."

"And if I don't return?" Freddy asked.

"Then we'll care for Michael as if he were one of our own," Ryan replied.

"You're really disappointing me," Janie snarled. Her eyes cut a hard stare at Ryan, who sat in the chair, head drooped, and expression of defeat written all over his face.

"I'll take that deal," Freddy said.

"Are you sure?" Janie asked.

"Just take care of Michael and help me bury James and Kayleigh," Freddy said.

"Are you sure?" Janie asked.

"Yes."

"Okay."

Freddy turned to head to the backyard to dig the graves when Ryan called out, "Hold up."

Freddy stopped. "Yeah."

"I'm really sorry about what happened. I mean, with Katy and Kayleigh and also with...framing you. You have to understand, I didn't have a choice."

"Everyone has a choice," Freddy said.

"But they were going to hurt my family," Ryan countered.

Freddy stared at Ryan's bruised face, the cuts still swollen and fresh from the beating he'd given him. "Why didn't you just come to me for help? We could have figured out something."

"The only thing we could have done was go and kill those bastards then. You know how the law works. What exactly could we have done?"

"Something better than framing me for murder," Freddy shot back.

"If I knew you could've helped me, I would have asked."

"When you and I are working together, we can accomplish a lot."

Ryan shook his head. "Fritz, you don't understand."

"Then make me."

"You were different back then. You were by the book. If this Fritz was there, you and I would've gone out and taken care of business."

"But that would've been against –"

Stopping Freddy by holding up his hand, Ryan said, "I know, against the law. You see, I had no way out. I had to do what I had to do."

"You know something, I forgive you. I remember when you asked me how far I'd go to protect my family, and I replied that I'd do anything. Now I know why you asked."

"I was struggling then. I had to make a choice."

Freddy put his hand on Ryan's shoulder and said, "You've always been a good friend up until you screwed me over, but that's the past. You watching over Michael...well, let's just say that we're even. You don't have me to worry about anymore."

"Thank you," Ryan said.

"But, Ryan, let me be clear. If in between now and my return, you do something to stab me in the back again, I'll kill you with my bare hands."

13

DECEMBER 9, 2014

DE LAROSA RESIDENCE, SOUTH SIDE, CHICAGO

ANTONIO TRIED TO STAY AWAKE, but the fatigue from multiple days of being on the go nonstop took its toll. Armed with his pistol, he curled up on the couch in the living room and fell asleep.

An unusual noise jolted him awake. He sat up and looked around, but his eyes could not see a thing. The candle he had been using had gone out, leaving him in the pitch-black dark. "Who's there?" he called out, his head swiveling on his shoulders back and forth, with his eyes desperately trying to see. "Is that you, Agent Becker?"

Silence.

After a minute he calmed himself down and went to lie down when he heard what sounded like a breath. Again, he shot up from the couch, this time pointing his pistol in the direction of the sound and pulling the trigger. The concussion from the single gunshot was loud. "Who's there?"

Silence.

Instead of lying back down, he got to his feet and slowly walked towards the table where he'd had the candle lit. He felt around blindly until he found the lighter. He lit the lighter. The orange flame illuminated the space. The dancing flame flickered.

He turned around and found himself face-to-face with Freddy. Startled, he jumped back.

Freddy was on him quickly. With two swift moves he disarmed him of the pistol and tossed it aside.

Antonio hadn't been defeated yet though. He put the lit lighter to Freddy's face.

The flame seared Freddy's face; however, he too wasn't deterred. He grabbed Antonio, lifted him up, and threw him on the table.

The weight of Antonio crashing into the table caused it to break apart.

With the flame from the lighter out, the house was plunged back into darkness.

Scrambling to get to his feet, Antonio rolled to his knees and went to rise, but somehow Freddy had found him.

Freddy had the sheath knife in his right hand and took full advantage of the situation. He slid the knife into Antonio's side, pulled it out, and slid it in again.

Antonio howled in pain. Using all his might, he swung his elbows back, hoping one would make contact and knock Freddy off.

After stabbing Antonio twice, Freddy was ready to deliver

the final blow. He held the knife high over his head and was about to plunge it deep into Antonio's back when an elbow caught him in the side. The blow was enough to unsteady Freddy and allow Antonio to slither out.

Frantic, Antonio crawled across the floor and into the kitchen.

Freddy stood. He tried to see, but it was impossible. "You're a dead man, De LaRosa."

Blood oozed from Antonio's sides. He'd been hurt bad but not enough to take him out of the fight. He got to his feet and felt around the counters for something he could fight with.

Fighting in the dark wasn't ideal, and Freddy couldn't take the chance of walking into a darkened room. He removed a flashlight from his back pocket and clicked it on.

The bright LED beam chased the darkness away and showed Freddy the bloody trail that led into the kitchen.

Browning Residence, Chicago

Janie gently closed the door of the bedroom Michael was sleeping in, and followed the glow of the candlelight to the kitchen. She heard packages being moved, and was curious as to what Ryan was up to. "He's asleep," she said, walking into the kitchen to find Ryan rummaging through one of the wagons. "What are you doing?"

Ryan looked up with shock at seeing her.

"You look as if I just caught you with your hand in the cookie jar."

"I, ah..."

"Wait, what are you doing?" she asked, seeing he had taken the large tubs of dehydrated food out of the wagon and had set them aside.

"We don't have enough."

"I know, but we'll find more."

He rushed up to her, his eyes wide. Taking her hands, he said, "Janie, I need you to trust me."

"You're going to steal their food!"

"There's two of them and four of us. We need it, and I don't know what we'll run into out there," he replied defensively.

"Wait, are you going to steal it and take off?"

"He won't let me have it."

"What has gotten into you?"

Looking at her with pleading eyes, he said, "Tell me how you're going to explain to the boys if we don't find any other food in a week? Tell me."

"But this isn't –"

"I'm tired of hearing what's right and wrong. Those are the morals of the old world. Right now we're living in a new one, and the only thing that's right is taking care of my family."

She pulled away from him and paced the room, her right hand planted on her forehead in deep thought.

"Tell me...huh? Tell me exactly what you plan on saying to the boys when they're begging to eat, when they're starving?"

"But it can't be that bad out there, it can't be. What you're saying sounds so...so crazy."

"Crazy? Look around you. Wake up, Janie. We just buried Kayleigh and James next to Katy in the freaking backyard. There are roving gangs killing and raping, and Freddy, Mr. Law and Order, just left to go murder a man."

She felt her knees get weak. Not wanting to fall, she went to the table and sat down. "You're right."

Relief washed over his face. He melted into the chair next to her. Taking her hands, he softly said, "I think we should take the entire wagon."

"But will they have enough?"

"They have another, and it's fully loaded as well."

"But this means we will need to leave Michael," she said.

"I know."

"But what if he doesn't return? What will happen to Michael?"

"Janie, we need to think of our own boys."

"This...I don't know, Ry, this just doesn't feel right."

"This is a matter of survival now, and if we're going to make it past a week, we need all of this food."

"I feel sick," she said, putting her face in her hands.

Feeling he had the upper hand, he got up, loaded everything back into the wagon, and wheeled it to the front door. He came back into the kitchen to find she was still as he left her. He went to her side and tenderly touched her back. "I'm going to go get the boys."

Janie remained silent in her guilt.

De LaRosa Residence, South Side Chicago

Armed with a cleaver, Antonio cowered just inside the pantry. Blood kept pouring from his wounds, and he could already feel the loss of blood. The thought of his own demise now filled his mind, but also there was a determination to kill Freddy. *If I'm going to die, I'm taking him with me*, he thought.

Cautiously stepping into the kitchen, Freddy scanned the space, paying most attention to the trail of blood that led to a door in the corner of the room. A grin stretched across his face. He set the flashlight on the counter, its beam pointed at the pantry door, then approached, knife ready. Standing a foot away, he reached to open it, but before he could, it burst open.

Antonio leapt from the pantry. He took a wide swing with the cleaver but missed Freddy by a mile.

Freddy stepped to the side, grabbed the arm Antonio held the cleaver in and, with his knife-wielding hand, came down across Antonio's arm, slicing it wide open.

The massive gash cut to the bone.

Antonio screamed in pain, dropped the cleaver, and tried to make a run for it.

Thinking fast, Freddy grabbed Antonio by the back of the collar and yanked him to the floor. He straddled him quickly and plunged down with his knife.

Antonio stopped Freddy, the tip of the blade three inches from his sternum. Using all his strength, he pushed back but was only met with equal force.

"You're going to die!" Freddy yelled. Sweat dripped from his brow and onto Antonio's face.

Unable to reply, Antonio struggled to hold the blade back.

Using his advantage again, Freddy pressed his body weight down. The blade drew closer. It now hovered an inch and a half over Antonio's chest.

Antonio tried to push back, but he couldn't. He was growing weak from the blood loss.

Again, Freddy pushed down. The blade covered half the distance and was now only a little more than half an inch away from penetrating his skin.

Knowing his life was in the balance, Antonio used every ounce of strength he had.

The tip of the blade moved away from his chest.

Freddy knew he had him and was going to relish his victory. He grunted and pressed down as hard as he could.

Antonio was done, his strength sapped, allowing the blade to penetrate his sternum a half inch. He yelped in pain.

Freddy continued to press down.

The blade went further into Antonio's chest.

Knowing victory was at hand, Freddy leaned close to Antonio's face. He looked him in the eyes and said, "Die!"

Antonio gargled blood and opened his mouth to speak, but nothing came out. Blood poured from his open mouth, and his eyes wandered from Freddy and stared blankly at the ceiling.

"Argh!" Freddy hollered as he shoved the remaining length of the blade into Antonio's chest.

Antonio let out a gasp and died.

With the job done, Freddy sighed. They say there isn't reward in killing those who have killed your loved ones, but he'd disagree with them, as he felt pure satisfaction in avenging his family's lives.

He sat up and pulled the knife out. He looked down at Antonio's lifeless body and said, "Burn in hell." He wiped the blood on Antonio's shirt, sheathed the knife and stood. His mission was complete. He had killed the man responsible for so much pain and death, but had also completed his transition from cop to modern-day vigilante. There was no turning back. He was a new man in a new world, and he felt good.

Browning Residence, Chicago

Freddy heard the cries the second he entered the house. "Michael?" he called out as he ran from the front door down the hall.

Michael emerged from the room, his cheeks rosy, eyes puffy and tears streaming down his face. "Where were you?"

"I had to go somewhere," he said, dropping to a knee and embracing Michael. "Janie?"

No reply.

"Janie, Ryan?"

Silence.

"Is anyone else here?" Freddy asked.

Michael shook his head.

"It's fine. I'm here now."

"You left me alone," Michael whimpered.

"I didn't. Mr. and Mrs. Pettigrew were supposed to watch you." Concerned that something awful had occurred, he picked Michael up and searched the house. He quickly found the house empty, as Michael had said, along with a missing wagon and months of food. "Liars," he snarled under his breath.

"Are they gone?"

"Yeah, they're gone."

"Are you going to leave again?" Michael asked.

"No, son, I'm not going anywhere," he answered. He hugged Michael tightly. "I'm never leaving you again."

South Side, Chicago

Upon leaving James's house, the Pettigrews raced home, grabbed their belongings, and took off on their journey out of the city, hoping the dark of night would provide cover.

"I feel horrible," Janie said, her breath visible in the chilled air.

"I'm sure Freddy made it home. Michael will be fine," Ryan said.

"You don't know that. Maybe we should go back and get him," Janie countered. She was having the hardest time coming to a resolution with what they'd done.

"He'll be fine."

"No, he won't. If Freddy doesn't return, we've essentially killed Michael too."

"We killed Michael?" their son Ricky asked. His pace was slower than the others, leaving him feet behind.

"We didn't kill Michael. Now try to keep up," Ryan scolded.

"This isn't good. We're not good people, Ryan. Karma is going to get us," Janie stressed.

"There's no such thing as karma," Ryan mocked.

They marched a few more blocks and turned a corner to see the light of dawn arriving.

"I'm tired," their other son, Randy, whined.

"Maybe we should rest," Janie said.

"No. We're not stopping until we're out of the city," Ryan snapped.

"But that could be a while," Janie said.

"We're in a bad neighborhood. There's no stopping until we're clear of it. Now stop babying him."

Janie suddenly stopped.

Frustrated, Ryan spun around and hissed, "We're not stopping, now c'mon."

She raised her hand and pointed.

Ryan looked in the direction she was pointing and saw six men emerge from an old abandoned building.

"Turn around," Ryan ordered.

Janie didn't protest. She turned and let out a yelp. "Ryan, there's more."

Five men were approaching from behind. In their hands they had weapons of all sorts, firearms, pipes and sticks.

To either side of the Pettigrews were old four-story factories. They'd been abandoned for decades and now served as hideouts for gang members and shelter for the homeless.

"This way," Ryan barked. He had pulled his pistol and with his left hand waved for his family to run towards one of the abandoned buildings.

Taking Randy's and Ricky's hands, Janie took off, but stopped the second she saw men come from the building she was headed towards. "Ryan!" she wailed.

Whistles and catcalls came from the men, who now numbered over a dozen.

"Back off or I'll shoot!" Ryan hollered as he waved his pistol from one man to the next.

Laughter was their response.

In a naive attempt to show he meant what he said, he raised his pistol and fired a round.

The men stopped.

"Leave us alone and let us pass!" he commanded.

A single man stepped out from the others. "You gotta pay the toll."

"I'm a cop. You need to let me pass," Ryan hollered.

"A cop? Now the toll just got a lot higher," the man replied, taking a few steps closer.

"Stay back."

"Man, what do you think is going on here? Huh? You come into my territory and start yelling about being a cop. Ain't no one cares about cops and shit. In fact, you might have just made it worse."

"What do you want?" Ryan asked.

Randy and Ricky started to cry while Janie consoled them.

"What do you have there?"

"Food, equipment…"

"And a pretty white woman." The man snickered.

Angered, Ryan leveled his pistol in the direction of the man. "Let us pass."

"You can shoot me; go ahead. You'll never make it out of here alive."

"I'll leave the wagons, but let us go."

The man approached slowly, his hands up and palms out to show he wasn't armed.

"Stay where you are!" Ryan barked.

"I need to see what you have; I can't accept this as a toll if it ain't what we want," the man said.

"It's food and other equipment, ah, a tent, sleeping bags."

"And what do I need with a tent? Do you think I'm going camping? Man, you're stupid." The man laughed.

"Just take it and let us pass." Ryan kept his pistol raised. He knew that after firing the one round, he only had another ten left, not enough to kill each one. "We're going this way. Just take it."

The man took a few more steps and stopped. "Go ahead."

"Let's go, hurry," Ryan said to Janie.

The four turned and ran in the direction they'd seen the first six men, who were still there. When they were feet from them, the men attacked. They knocked Janie and the boys to the ground and took hold of Ryan.

Ryan fired a single shot but didn't hit a thing. He struggled but was quickly overwhelmed, his pistol knocked out of his hand.

The man, who must have been their leader, walked up and looked down on Ryan with a sneer. The man had a thick scar diagonally across his cheek. He picked up Ryan's pistol from the ground, put it to Ryan's head, and pulled the trigger without a second thought. "Fucking cop."

Janie shrieked in terror and the boys sobbed.

The man turned and shot Randy and Ricky dead. He bent down, grabbed Janie's face, and said, "Ain't you a pretty little thang. Take her back to my place."

Janie kicked and wailed, but her efforts were fruitless.

"Grab the rest of their shit and divide it up. If there's anything good, let me know." He watched as Janie was dragged off, her screams echoing off the eroding structures. "Stupid motherfuckers, what were they thinking coming into my territory."

Another man walked up. "What about the bodies?"

"Leave them where they lie," the man said and strutted off. He thought for a minute then said, "Actually, hang them from them light posts at the border of my territory. Place signs warning people that this is what happens when you don't pay the toll."

HAVING a single wagon helped with the logistics of hauling, as Michael wouldn't have been able to pull one himself. The Pettigrews had taken most of the dehydrated food, but there was still enough that would last them a couple of months. Enough to get them to Lake of the Ozarks, at least he hoped.

"How long are we going to walk for?" Michael asked, the morning sun warming his chilled face.

"As long as it takes," Freddy answered. "We'll take a good long break once we get out of the city, okay?"

"Okay."

They continued to walk in silence. Only the whip of the wind coming off Lake Michigan could be heard.

Freddy had his rifle slung, and his head was on a swivel. He saw people coming and going, but no one paid him heed. Like the early days, the sound of gunfire could be heard, but he did notice it wasn't as prevalent as before.

"Daddy, look, it's Mr. Pettigrew," Michael said, his finger pointing down the street.

Freddy instantly stopped. His eyesight clearly wasn't as good as Michael's, 'cause he saw the body hanging from the light post; however, he couldn't quite make out who it was. "Are you sure?"

"Yeah, it's him. I think he's dead."

Cautiously Freddy advanced so he could read the sign hung around Ryan's neck. When it came into view, he stopped and read.

He didn't pay the toll / no cops allowed.

"It's him, isn't it?" Michael asked.

"Yeah," Freddy said, turning the wagon around and heading west down the cross street away from Ryan's hanging body.

"Daddy?"

"Yeah."

"Will that happen to us?"

"Not a chance, buddy, not a chance."

The two walked for miles. Street after street they went until they cleared the city limits and entered the suburbs. There they found the same carnage. Freddy didn't know exactly what would lie ahead, but he had a good guess they'd find more of the same. He'd been through a lot, but he wasn't anywhere close to giving up.

EPILOGUE

"Are we there yet?" Michael asked.

Taking a chance to stop, not because he wanted to answer Michael's question but due to a heavy fatigue that was washing over Freddy, he craned his head back and replied, "Not even close."

"I'm hungry," Michael whined as he adjusted in the wagon.

Freddy knew Michael was restless, he was too, they'd been on the road hiking for a couple of weeks now.

"Are we going to camp out again?"

"Well, buddy, we may have to on account hotels sorta went out of business a few weeks ago. But, God, what I'd do for a Best Western right now."

"Why can't we stay in a house? There's so many. Can't someone let us sleep there?" Michael innocently asked.

Freddy wanted nothing else but to find a warm bed and get out of the cold, especially after the snowstorm they'd just dealt with days before. "We don't know those people."

"Why not knock?"

Freddy opened his mouth to counter the question when the thought came to him. *Why not just knock?* He scanned the rural area, nothing around him but dead dried stalks of corn and patches of old crusty snow. In the distance he caught the glimmer of something reflecting in the afternoon sun's waning rays. "Hmm," he mused. "How about we go see if they have a bed that they'd let us sleep in?"

"Yeah," Michael cheered, his cheeks rosy from the cold.

The two made their way down the deserted county road to the long gravel drive. At the end an older two-story farmhouse stood, its covered porch teasing them to come.

"I don't see any smoke coming out of the chimney," Freddy said.

"Then no one is home, next house," Michael said.

"No, we'll try this one," Freddy said, giving the wagon a tug.

They cautiously made their way down the long drive, with Freddy carefully scanning the windows to ensure no one was ready and waiting to gun them down. Each step he took closer, he felt more confident that no one was there.

The property itself was large, with the two-story house and three outbuildings: a barn and two small wooden sheds.

"Hello!" Freddy called out, his hands in the air to show he

was not carrying, although his sidearm was easily accessible and an AR-platform rifle he'd recently acquired was slung across his back.

No response nor movement from the house or other buildings.

"No one is home," Michael said, his eyes also scrutinizing the house.

"I don't think so," Freddy said. He faced Michael and said, "I'm going to approach the house. You stay here. If you see someone, holler out."

"Okay."

Freddy tousled Michael's hair, winked and said, "You're a good boy."

"I'll make sure the wagon is safe," Michael said.

A smile cracked Freddy's rugged face. He could see Kaitlyn's eyes, something that warmed him to see each time he looked at him.

A stiff wind swept over them, sending a chill down their backs.

"I'm cold."

Looking back to the house, Freddy said, "Maybe we'll find a warm bed in there. Now stay put, and don't forget to holler if you see anyone."

"Okay."

The frozen gravel crunched under Freddy's weight each step he took. He no longer was empty handed, his rifle now firmly in his grip.

He reached the worn wooden steps, which led to the wraparound porch, and paused to look at the old crusty snow still there. He was struck that no footprints were present, something he also noticed on the porch itself. This told him no one was home, at least not since it had snowed recently. He scaled the steps. The boards underneath him creaked with each step. "Hello!" he called out.

No response.

He reached for the front door but paused when he noticed what looked like the silhouette of a person near the front window. He raised his rifle and took a step closer to find it was a person, but whoever they were, they had been dead a while.

He peered through the window, to discover it was a man. In his lap was a pistol, and by the dark stain on the wall behind him, he could easily tell the man had shot himself in the head.

"Dad, I'm cold," Michael cried out.

Not looking back, Freddy replied, "I need a few more minutes to clear the house. Just sit tight." Freddy advanced to the door, turned the knob, to find it unlocked, and pushed it open. A stale and pungent odor wafted over him. He recoiled, lifted a bandana he had around his neck to cover his nose and mouth, and entered the house.

"I don't mean you any harm!" he again called out just in case someone else was there, though he doubted it. He made his way to the dead man's body and discovered a note scribbled with one sentence. *Hell is open, and all the devils are here.*

"Sorry, buddy," Freddy said and tossed the note aside. Not one to just let a firearm sit around, he picked it up, press-checked it, and slid it into his thick overcoat.

"Is he dead?" Michael asked.

Startled, Freddy spun around. "I told you to wait in the wagon."

"I have to pee. Plus I'm cold."

Freddy swept Michael up and marched him back outside. "You have to listen to me, do you understand?"

Michael nodded.

"Do you?"

"Yes."

"You do as I say, all the time. The world is a dangerous place. You have to listen to my commands, or something..." Freddy said but stopped short of telling him the gruesome consequences.

"If I don't listen, I'll die like Mommy and –"

"Stop."

"Is he dead?"

"Yes."

"Did someone kill him?"

"He killed himself."

"Why?"

Freddy sighed. "We will discuss this later. Go get the wagon and bring it inside. I'm going to clean this up, and together we will search the house."

"Okay," Michael said, rushing away.

Freddy walked back inside, looked at the dead man, and said, "Let's go find a place to put you."

AS FREDDY HAD THOUGHT, the house was empty save for the body of the man. He didn't know what had driven the man to such desperation, but it wasn't a lack of resources, as the pantry was filled with food stores and potable water stored in the garage in large drums. He felt like he'd won the lottery, a fortune of luck that spared him normally.

He and Michael ate well, and soon he put him to bed. As he stood over him, he longed for the days of old, but they were never coming back. He and Michael now belonged to the present, to a new world, and what lay ahead of them down the road was a mystery.

Buried in the stash of food, he'd found a nice bottle of whiskey and intended to enjoy a glass or two before he too went to bed.

In the glow of a kerosene lantern he'd found in one of the sheds, he poured several fingers' worth of whiskey and leaned back, the chair squeaking under his weight.

Just as he was about to kick his legs up, he saw a radio. "I wonder." He picked it up and noticed something was different. On the side was a crank. He put his glass down and cranked a few turns.

The radio came to life.

"Nice!" he said with wide eyes and excitement. He

cranked it as much as he could, then searched the airwaves, only to find static. Determined, he kept rolling through the airwaves, the distinct crackle and hum bringing back memories of his youth and his grandfather's old handheld wireless, until he hit pay dirt.

Stay tuned for a message from the President of the United States.

He sat up, curious as to what he'd just found and what the president would say. He took a long drink from his glass and waited.

My fellow Americans, this is President Conner. I am addressing you this Christmas night not to express holiday wishes but to inform you that another tragedy has befallen our great country. This morning, the enemies of the United States attacked New York City with a weapon of mass destruction. The information we have received so far is that many of our fellow citizens have paid the ultimate sacrifice and have perished in this heinous and cowardly attack.

Today's attack, along with the initial attacks three weeks ago, has prompted me to finally take action. This decision did not come lightly, but after much thought and prayer, I decided that we must finally act. I gave the order an hour ago for a full-scale nuclear retaliation against those who are responsible for the attacks against us. I can now report that our nuclear forces successfully struck targets within the following countries: Iran, Iraq, Syria, Yemen, Somalia, North Korea, Pakistan, Afghanistan, Egypt, Tunisia and Libya.

I believe this action was justified and will prevent these coun-

tries from conducting further attacks against us. Let me be clear to those who may be still out there who wish us harm. We will not just bring you to justice, we will destroy you. Do not tread on us!

I know the past three weeks have been extremely difficult, and your way of life is now different, but I can assure you that we are working tirelessly to get our power grid and infrastructure back online. In the meantime, we can help support you by food and medical shipments as we get them from our allies. Your government has not forgotten you.

So, as this Christmas comes to a close, we must all come together and remember that life is difficult right now, but we are Americans, and we, like others before us, will persevere through these dark times. We must not lose hope and must not give in. We will make it and we will rebuild, that I promise you...may God bless you and may God bless the United States of America.

The radio went silent.

"Whoa," Freddy said out loud, shocked by the speech he'd heard. He leaned back and processed what he'd just heard. It all seemed so surreal, as if he were living in a dream or, better yet, a nightmare. Regardless of what had happened, this was his new life. He hadn't even thought about it being Christmas; heck, he wasn't exactly looking at a calendar every day.

He tossed the drink back, turned down the flame, and headed to bed. Tomorrow was a new day in this new world, a world with a new set of rules, rules that required him to adapt or die. He had no choice. This wasn't just about him, but Michael. He'd find a way, a way to survive and hopefully thrive. As he had all his life, he'd take it a day at a time, pray for the best, and expect the worst.

THE END

ABOUT THE AUTHOR

L. Douglas Hogan is a U.S.M.C. veteran with over twenty years in public service. Among these are three years as an anti-tank infantryman, one year as a Marine Corps Marksmanship Instructor, ten years as a part-time police officer, and twenty years working in state government doing security work and supervision. He has been married over twenty-five years, has two children, and is faithful to his church, where he resides in southern Illinois.

His Facebook page is www.facebook.com/HonorYourOath

His newsletter sign-up and website is at www. LDouglasHogan.com

ABOUT THE AUTHOR

G. Michael Hopf is a USA Today Bestselling author of almost forty novels including the international bestselling post-apocalyptic series, THE NEW WORLD. He has made a prominent name for himself in both the post-apocalyptic and western genres. To date he has sold over one million copies of his books worldwide and many of his works have been translated into German, French and Spanish.

He is the co-founder of BEYOND THE FRAY PUBLISHING and DOOMSDAY PRESS and a veteran of the United States Marine Corps. He lives with his family in San Diego, CA.

Contact him at geoff@gmichaelhopf.com with any questions or comments. www.gmichaelhopf.com

www.facebook.com/gmichaelhopf

www.twitter.com/gmichaelhopf